ARENA OF SHAME

by

KATE BENEDICT

Published by **CHIMERA**
ISBN 9781780806655

CHAPTER 1

'Help me! Please, help me!' Branna pleaded, but the fleeing tribesmen were deaf to her cries. Stunned by defeat, and intent only on their own escape, the line of weary men passed the young woman struggling to right the toppled cart without a second glance.

Branna stared at them with frightened eyes. The last remnants of Boudicca's proud army, they were a sorry sight to behold. Bloodstained and filthy, they limped past in an unending stream, some clutching wounds bound up with makeshift bandages, some using their spears as crutches, and some hobbling beneath the weight of wounded comrades. She gasped and averted her eyes as one man, half his face gone, staggered past her bent double beneath the body of a son or a brother, his one remaining eye staring blindly out from around a mask of blood.

Her mouth set as she turned her attention back to the fallen cart. Taking a deep breath, she set her shoulder to the wheel and pushed with all her strength in an effort to right it. Her feet slid in the muddy earth, and the cart remained exactly where it was. Straightening up again, she aimed a vicious kick at it. Yet even if she managed to right it, there was no way she could move it now that her small shaggy pony was gone; she was sure someone had eaten him.

'Leave it,' a harsh voice commanded, and she looked up to see a man older than her father gesticulating urgently. 'Run, girl, get out of here before the Romans come!'

The Romans! Her stomach clenched with the strength of her hatred. *Curse them! Curse them all!* She spat on the ground. It was not enough to grind her tribe into poverty with their taxes and their moneylenders; they had to have it all. When King Prasutagas died without a male heir, they used this as an excuse to seize everything. And when Queen Boudicca protested, they scourged her within an inch of her life and ravished her daughters before her very eyes.

Branna closed her own eyes against the memory of the day when she had been forced to watch her queen beaten like a common criminal and her daughters publicly abused and dishonoured. Even now she shuddered remembering the echo of their screams mingling with the jeers and catcalls of the soldiers. But they had paid for that, and they had paid dearly. Boudicca had been magnificent as she called her tribe to arms. With her long tawny hair falling to her waist, a thick golden torque gleaming around her neck and her cloak billowing in the wind, her words could have inspired the dead to rise. And they had not been alone in their fight. The Trinovantes had joined them, and together they marched against the might of Rome, and won. Andastra, goddess of victory, had favoured them. Camolodunum, with its hated temple to Claudius, had fallen first, the ninth legion defeated, with only its cavalry escaping. Londinium had fallen next, and then Verulamium. The skies had been alight with fires that burned for days and nights as everything was destroyed, and the shrieks of dying Romans had been music to the ears.

It had been a glorious adventure and she, Branna, had been part of it. She could not possibly have stayed at home in the safety of the *oppida* when the world was on the move. Despite her mother's wailing and hand wringing, she joined the other women who chose to follow their husbands, sons and lovers to battle.

Her face softened as she thought of Cerdoc, her betrothed. How fine he looked with his blue eyes ablaze with excitement. 'We'll show them,' he had told her, 'and with the booty I gather, we can buy sheep and cattle for our farm. And you shall have a fine belt and an embroidered tunic for your wedding day, and a mirror, too!'

There was no time for a wedding, but in the eyes of Teutates they were one already. They had shared a makeshift bed beneath the stars, and his strong body had pleasured hers. Her lips parted as she grew breathless remembering their lovemaking... the feel of his chest against her breasts and the strength of his thighs and buttocks... the heat and hardness of his manhood as it slid inside her... she closed her eyes and shivered, remembering how she moaned and writhed beneath him, her hips bucking as she met each of his thrusts with one of her own, until they shuddered to release together...

A heavy hand falling on her shoulder startled Branna back to reality, and she found herself staring up into the angry face of the old man who had urged her to run. 'Are you mad, girl?' he demanded, shaking her roughly. 'Do you want to fall into the hands of the Romans? Have you any idea what they'll do to you? Take what you can and run while you still have the chance.'

Her chin rose as she stared back at him defiantly. 'I go nowhere without my man. I shall wait here until he returns.'

'Teutates give me strength,' he groaned. 'If the ravens are picking his eyes, you'll have a long wait. Or are you going to stand here until *Samhain* when he comes back from the dead?'

She stared at him in dismay. The thought that Cerdoc might be dead had not even crossed her mind, and now she shook it off stubbornly. How could that strong young body, so warm and full of life, be lying cold on a battlefield? It was impossible. 'I shall wait for my man,' she repeated firmly, pulling a small knife from her girdle. 'And if he is dead, then I shall follow him into the next world.'

'So be it,' the old man said with grudging admiration. 'We must all make our own choices, and I choose to live.' He nodded at her in farewell, and rejoined the rest of his fleeing comrades.

Branna watched him until he disappeared beneath the trees, and then she turned her attention back to the cart. If she could not salvage it, then she would take whatever she could carry. Pulling a small skin from the back, she began to pile their few remaining supplies onto it. It was a motley collection - a few strips of cloth, a wad of the healing moss used to pack wounds, some dried meat, a lump of hard cheese and a hunk of even harder bread. Then there were Cerdoc's spoils - a scattering of coins, a lump of amber on a thin silver chain, and a ring dented as it was chopped off the finger of a dead body. She sighed as she tied up the corners of her bundle, and hefted it experimentally over one shoulder. At least it would be easy to carry.

She set the bundle down, wrapped her cloak around her against the rain, and sat on the edge of the cart anxiously scanning the faces of the passing men. Twice she leapt to her feet and twice she sank down again in disappointment, as the man she thought was Cerdoc proved to be a stranger.

At last an undeniably familiar figure stumbled into the clearing, and her heart leapt into her mouth as she took in his condition. His clothes were torn and stained with blood, a long gash down his right arm was still dripping blood despite the strip of cloth he had ripped from his cloak to tie around it, and his face was a mask of exhaustion beneath a soiled mane of hair. Dropping her bundle, Branna ran towards him.

'What are you still doing here?' he demanded, gripping one of her shoulders with his good hand. 'I thought you safely gone!'

'Did you think I would go without you?' she replied scornfully. 'Did you think I would run away like a frightened girl? I am Iceni,' she added proudly, 'not some simpering Roman maiden.' She pulled him towards the cart. 'Come and sit down while I tend to your wound.'

'There's no time,' he argued frantically. 'They're right behind me. Can't you hear them? In the name of Teutatis, leave me and run while you still have a chance!'

She froze, her ears straining for sounds of the enemy even as she forced a smile. 'I hear nothing,' she lied, shaking her head, and ran to pick up her bundle. 'Come,' she said gently but firmly, 'put your arm around my shoulder. We can move more quickly if you lean on me.'

Too exhausted to argue, Cerdoc did as he was told, and together they stumbled into the dark maw of the forest.

At first it seemed as if fate was on their side. Taranis growled overhead, and the mists thickened until they could barely see anything. Faint despairing shrieks audible in the distance told them the Romans had come upon some other unfortunate refugees, and Branna hoped the old man who had tried his best to save her was not one of them.

Eventually, even these sounds died away and all they heard was water dripping from leaves and the nervous scuffling of small animals in the undergrowth. Then darkness fell, bringing with it an illusion of safety.

She let her heavy bundle drop to the waterlogged ground, and looked around them. She could hear a stream running through the small clearing they found themselves in. 'This will do as well as anywhere to spend the night,' she said. 'Even if we dare not start a fire, we will at least have fresh water. There is enough dried meat and cheese left for tonight, and we can hunt for fresh meat tomorrow when we are rested.' She looked anxiously at Cerdoc. 'Now sit down and let me tend your wound.'

With a groan of exhaustion, he slumped down at the foot of a tree and allowed her to unwind the filthy cloth from around his arm, gritting his teeth against the pain. Hiding her dismay at the sight of his swollen flesh, she washed it with icy water from the stream, packed the gash with healing moss, and bound it tightly again with clean strips of cloth torn from her own cloak. Finally, she sat back on her heels and smiled at him. 'There,' she said with forced cheerfulness, 'I think I caught it before it poisoned.'

'And at least it wasn't my sword arm,' he added.

Much to her relief, the colour was returning to his lips. Once he had some food in his belly, it would help replace the blood he had lost, and a good night's sleep would set his feet on the path to recovery in no time. She began to feel more optimistic; they were both alive, they had escaped their enemies, and tomorrow they would put even more distance between themselves and their pursuers. Humming beneath her breath, she untied her bundle and drew out the remains of the food, dividing it so Cerdoc had the larger share.

Then, after they had eaten, she gathered bracken, piled it beneath some overhanging bushes, and laid the skin on top of it to form a makeshift bed.

'Come,' she urged, smiling in the darkness. 'We must sleep. Wrapped in each other's arms, and with our cloaks about us, we should be warm enough.'

4

'If it wasn't for this arm of mine, I'd soon heat you up,' he replied, slipping his good arm around her waist.

'I said sleep,' she scolded him, pushing him away gently. 'You must save your strength for the morrow. There'll be time enough for that when we're out of harm's way.'

Grumbling in mock protest, he allowed her to help him down, and then she stood over him for a long moment straining her ears for any sounds of movement. When she heard none, she lay down beside him, pulled their cloaks around them, and curled up against his side, carefully avoiding his wounded arm. Slowly, the damp chill left their exhausted bodies, and they fell into a fitful sleep.

Three times Branna started awake in terror, once to the high-pitched screech of an owl swooping down on unsuspecting prey, a second time to the distant howling of wolves, and a third time to the snorting of a wild boar as it charged through the undergrowth nearby.

When dawn finally arrived she arose heavy-eyed, her limbs leaden and aching.

Cerdoc was still sleeping heavily, moaning and muttering to himself. Looking down at him, she bit her lip anxiously. His pallor had been replaced by an unhealthy flush, and the flesh above and below his bound wound was red and swollen. She would let him keep resting while she went downstream to attend to her bodily needs, and then she would see if she could find some mushrooms, or even a rabbit, if she was lucky. If it still felt safe they might risk a fire, and if not, blood and raw meat were unappetising but nourishing.

Covering him with his cloak again, she checked the dagger in her belt and walked quietly away from the clearing.

She had no luck with the hunting, but she did find a few edible fungi. Scooping up her skirt, she bent over and began gathering them, and so engrossed was she in her task that she spun around with a cry of surprise when she suddenly felt a heavy hand grip her shoulder.

'What have we got here?' A Roman legionary grinned at her. 'A tasty little morsel to start the day with, I'd say,' he added, answering his own stupid question.

She did not understand all his words, but the look in his eyes made his intentions clear. Her hand flew to the dagger at her belt - but too late.

He got there first, snatched the weapon away from her, and tossed it to one of his comrades. 'That's no way to treat conquering heroes,' he chided her, reaching out and squeezing one of her breasts. 'You want to be nice to us. Doesn't she, boys?'

Panting in fear, Branna looked around the circle of faces and saw lust written on all five of them. Certain they would slake their desire on her helpless body, then cut her throat and leave her to rot, desperation gave her strength. She brought her right knee up and rammed it into the leader's groin, wrenching herself free of his grip as she did so and taking to her heels. There was a moment of stunned silence as his companions watched him double up, clutching himself and groaning in pain, but then they ran after her, whooping and yelling angrily.

Ignoring the branches whipping and snatching at her, Branna ran towards the clearing, and Cerdoc. 'Quick!' she cried as he staggered to his feet. 'We have to get out of here. Run!'

The first of the legionaries burst into the clearing, saw Cerdoc, and reached for his sword.

Shoving Branna behind him, Cerdoc pulled out his own sword and fell into a fighting crouch, holding the deadly blade out before him.

The other soldiers arrived, their leader limping along in the rear, and exchanged sly smiles. One wounded man and an unarmed girl against six of Rome's finest. It would be over in moments. They surrounded the two Iceni, stabbing playfully at Cerdoc with their short-swords like cats toying with a mouse.

'Mind the girl,' the leader grunted. 'I've got plans for that little bitch.'

Cerdoc had done enough trading in the *oppida* to understand the man's words, and he was an Iceni warrior. He lunged furiously at the soldier nearest him, and the point of his blade sank through the leather breast-guard into the soft flesh beneath. The Roman gave him a look of sheer astonishment, and fell facedown on the boggy ground, dead.

All the playfulness vanished from his companions' eyes, which regarded the blond barbarian with new respect even as they rushed him. Cerdoc fought like a madman, but he was borne down under the weight of numbers while Branna shrieked and flew at his attackers, her fingers hooked into claws, but their desperate struggles were useless.

'Shall I kill the bastard now?' one of the panting soldiers demanded, the point of his sword held at Cerdoc's throat. Blood streamed down from the Iceni's reopened wound, but another Roman lay unconscious on the ground and the others had not emerged unscathed.

'Not yet,' their leader replied breathlessly. 'Let him watch while we show his woman what real men are like.' He grabbed the front of Branna's tunic, ripped it open, and licked his lips at the sight of her soft white breasts. He ran his hands over them, pinching her pink nipples.

'Go on, Maximus,' the one holding the sword at Cerdoc's throat urged, 'show her how you got your name.'

With an answering grin, Maximus flung her down across the ground, straddled her, hoisted his leather kilt, and fumbled out his swollen cock.

Cerdoc went mad. Wrenching himself free of his captors, he rammed his forehead into the Roman in front of him, smashing the man's nose into a bloody pulp. Then he whirled around, grabbed the one behind him by the throat with both hands, and began choking the life out of him. He had almost succeeded when the hilt of a sword thudded into the back of his skull, and he sank unconscious into a muddy puddle. For a few moments the clearing was filled with the terrible thudding sound of fists and boots sinking into unprotected flesh as his senseless body was kicked and beaten.

Branna closed her eyes in despair. Her lover was dead. No man could withstand punishment like that, particularly when he was already wounded, and survive.

'Now, where was I?' Maximus asked, smirking down at her. 'Ah yes.' He spat on his hand, and rubbed his prick until the bulbous purple tip looked as if it would burst. Then he threw up her skirt, wrenched her thighs apart, and thrust two fingers into her soft pussy.

Branna bit back a cry; she would not give them the satisfaction of seeing her pain. The sooner they finished with her and cut her throat, the sooner she could join Cerdoc in the next world.

The soldier withdrew his fingers, and then thrust them in again, grinning as she defiantly held his stare. Then she gasped as he threw himself across her, his weight and the stench of his sweat nearly knocking the breath out of her. She could feel his cockhead pushing at the entrance to her body, and braced herself for the penetration.

But it did not come.

Suddenly the soldier's weight was lifted off her, and she could breathe again. Stunned, she opened her eyes and saw a tall, hard-faced man standing over her, his hands on his hips as he glared at her tormentors. His uniform did not look any different from theirs, but he was obviously a figure of authority. She struggled to remember the term... *centurion*.

'And exactly what do you think you're playing at, Maximus?' the newcomer demanded angrily. 'I send you out to forage, and this is what you find?'

'A prisoner, sir,' muttered Maximus. His prick had shrivelled to nothing, and he was trying to stand to attention and tuck it away at the same time. Under different circumstances, Branna would have found the sight very amusing.

'A prisoner?' the centurion snapped. 'This slip of a girl?'

'Iceni, sir, one of the rebels, and her man killed poor Gaius before we finished him off. She deserves whatever she gets.'

The centurion glanced indifferently at Cerdoc's body, and then looked thoughtfully down at Branna. 'In that case,' he stabbed a finger at two of the soldiers, 'you, and you, bind her, escort her to camp, and put her in my tent. She should bring a few sesterces in Rome.' He glared at them. 'And if you lay so much as a finger on her, I'll have your guts for garters.'

'But, sir,' Maximus protested, 'I found her first, so she's mine. Spoils of war.'

His superior grinned nastily. 'When you're a centurion, then you'll be entitled to the spoils of war. Until then, keep your mouth shut and do as you're told.'

'Yes, sir,' Maximus muttered, looking down at his boots.

The sound of a horse whinnying froze them all in place as a young man rode into the clearing. Branna gaped at him in wonder. His armour was so highly polished the early morning sun breaking through the rolling clouds shone off it almost blindingly, and whereas the men on the ground were grimy and battle-worn, he looked as if he had just stepped out of a bathhouse. He leaned on the pommel of his saddle and grinned down at the stunned group.

'I think we'll have her sent to *my* tent, centurion,' he drawled. 'A pretty girl like that would be wasted on the likes of you.'

'Yes, prefect,' the centurion replied stiffly.

'Good, now be about your business. I want as many stragglers caught and killed as possible. We don't want another rebellion, do we?'

'No, prefect,' the centurion remained at attention, his face blank, until his superior rode away, and then he spat on the ground. 'Bastard!' he muttered. He whirled around on the others. 'And you can wipe those bloody smirks off your faces. Do as the man said, otherwise there'll be trouble.'

Clutching her torn tunic over her breasts, Branna got stiffly to her feet and glanced from face to face, trying to understand what was happening. As two grinning legionaries grabbed her arms and hustled her off, she gazed despairingly over her shoulder at Cerdoc's body, until the trees hid her dead lover from view forever.

Meanwhile, the centurion walked over and nudged Cerdoc's body with his foot. 'Not bad fighters, the Iceni,' he remarked with grudging admiration. 'Shame they rebelled.

The empire could do with a few more like him.'

There was a groan, and Cerdoc's eyes flickered open. For a moment he fumbled on the ground for his sword, and then lapsed into unconsciousness again.

'Zeus protect us, he's till alive!' Maximus exclaimed. He knelt beside the body and reached for his dagger. 'Well, I'll soon fix that.'

'No,' the centurion snapped. 'Take him away and tend to his wounds. If he survives, I can find a use for him.'

'And if he doesn't?'

'In that case,' he said indifferently, 'throw his carcass on the midden with the rest of the carrion.'

Dazed with grief, Branna lost track of time as she stumbled along between her captors. Exhausted by emotion and by lack of food, she staggered and nearly fell several times, and barely noticed when the men used the excuse of steadying her to caress her. Life was reduced to the struggle of putting one leaden foot in front of the other.

When they stopped to camp that night, she collapsed onto the wet ground and sat rocking back and forth, her cloak wrapped around her. She was so cold, and Cerdoc's body would be cold now, too, his limbs stiff with death, and the thought of him lying alone and comfortless, with no one's love and prayers to guide him safely into the next world, was more than she could bear. She bit her lip to stop herself from bursting into sobs and sat bolt upright, her head held high as she glared at her two captors. She was Iceni, and she was damned if she was going to give the bastards the satisfaction of breaking her.

The Romans ignored her as they set up camp with the brisk efficiency of long practice. She watched with pretended apathy as they gathered wood, and started a fire. Perhaps they would let down their guard and she could make a break for it. If she ran for the woods she might find a deer path while they blundered through the undergrowth after her...

Very casually she stood up, stretching and yawning as if she was merely easing her aching muscles. She took a step backwards and nothing happened, so she took another step. She was bracing herself to turn and run for the trees when a strong hand gripped her arm, and she was flung back down onto the ground.

'Oh no you don't, my pretty, you stay right where you are. Prefect Paulus wants you taken to camp, and that's exactly where you're going. I'm not risking my pay because you fancied a little stroll in the woods.'

She glared up at the guard, panting with rage and frustration.

He smiled, eyeing the glimpse of soft breasts beneath her torn tunic. 'Pity he put you off limits,' he muttered. 'I could do with a nice little piece to warm my bedroll.' He ran his tongue over his lips. 'Saving you for himself, he is, the greedy swine.' His gaze became cunning. 'Still, who's to tell him... you?' He laughed. 'Not when you can't speak a word of a decent, civilised tongue.'

A quiver of fear ran through Branna and she pulled her cloak tightly about her. She knew enough to guess his intentions as he took another step towards her.

'Better not, mate,' his companion said regretfully. 'Not if you fancy keeping the skin on your back. I wouldn't mind a helping or two myself, but Paulus isn't going to take too kindly to you disobeying his orders.'

'Bitch!' the first man hissed in disappointment. 'She's probably diseased anyway. I hope his cock falls off.' Branna gasped as he aimed a kick at her and caught her a glancing blow in the ribs. Then he turned his back on her and returned to tending the cooking tin bubbling over the fire.

Hopelessness washed through her as her vision of freedom vanished. *If only she had died with Cerdoc!*

She had to force herself to eat when they fed her, the taste of captivity bitter on her tongue, and the sour wine washing it down might as well have been water for all the effect it had on her.

When it came time to bed down for the night, she hardly registered the humiliation of having to relieve herself while her captors watched, and sniggered. Producing a length of thin leather, they then tethered her to a tree like a leashed dog, flung a blanket at her, and pointed to the ground beside the fire. Obediently she spread herself across the blanket with hope springing anew inside her. Perhaps she could free herself while they were sleeping... but this brief hope was also quickly dashed. While one of the men wrapped himself in his blanket and curled up on the opposite side of the fire, the other stood guard, leaning on his short spear as he gazed into the night.

Sighing, Branna closed her eyes and let exhaustion claim her.

She woke to the smell of cooking. For a few blessed moments she was back with Cerdoc, and then reality crashed over her again and brought a flood of grief with it. She gasped in a pain both emotional and physical as a boot dug into her side.

'Get up, bitch, you've got another long walk ahead of you today.'

She sat up and pulled her cloak around her shoulders, again feeling the unwelcome pressure of her bladder. In a mixture of sign language and broken Latin, she indicated her need, and was glad when the smaller of the two men untied her leash and led her off into the bushes. She squatted, grateful that this time he had the decency to turn his back on her as she relieved herself.

She breakfasted on water, and a piece of flatbread still hot from the stones it was cooked on, while her captors broke their temporary camp. Then she was yanked unceremoniously to her feet.

'Get a move on.' The tall soldier shoved her forward so hard she nearly fell. 'We haven't got all day!'

Gathering the tattered remnants of her dignity around her, she cast one scathing glance back at him, and began walking.

It was evening, and the cooking fires were already beginning to burn, when they finally reached the main camp. Despite herself, Branna was impressed by its size, and for a while curiosity overcame her misery. This was the camp of her enemies and she wanted to despise them, yet she could not help but admire the signs of discipline she saw everywhere she looked.

A stockade surrounded the camp, and they were met at the gate by two guards who checked them thoroughly before permitting them to enter. Although she could not see them, she did not doubt other guards were posted around the perimeter. There was no chance of any of her fellow tribesmen attacking the camp under cover of nightfall; they would be cut down before they had gone a spear's length.

Row upon row of tents laid out in neat lines stretched into the darkness, and she was surprised there were no piles of ordure, and the overlying stench of human waste, she expected. No doubt the neat Romans had dug pits somewhere nearby. There was an air of cheerful good humour in the camp as the men relaxed after their victory, and bitterness washed over her again; there was no celebration for her people, who were all wounded and hiding in the hills and forests, or lying dead beneath a tree like her beloved Cerdoc.

There were wounds here, too, but they were all neatly bound, and no doubt the more serious cases were being tended to inside tents. All around her men were playing dice and drinking and turning cooking meat on makeshift spits. The more conscientious were tending to their equipment, sharpening swords and polishing shields. She heard the sound of hammer on metal, and saw one soldier beating the dents out of his breastplate.

As she passed the men looked up, grinned, and called out remarks she knew must be lewd because her captors kept laughing in response.

'Paulus said we couldn't touch, but he didn't say anything about looking,' her tall companion remarked. 'Let's give the boys a show.' He wrenched the concealing cloak from her shoulders, and yanked down the top of her tunic. The material, already torn, gave way and fell to her waist, revealing her plump breasts, their tips rosy in the firelight. When she tried to cover herself with her arms, he grabbed her wrists and pulled them behind her back. The movement thrust her bosom into prominence, and she blushed beneath a chorus of catcalls. Then her breasts bounced as she staggered forward, bringing more jeers from the soldiers, and despite her resolve, her courage began to dissolve. It seemed she must walk forever through the ranks of her tormentors. The flames lit their faces, glistening off wet lips, gleaming teeth and gaping mouths, and made them look like creatures from a nightmare.

It was a relief when her escorts eventually stopped in front of a tent considerably larger than the rest. A legionary in full armour stood before it, and he dropped his spear to bar the entrance and spat out something incomprehensible. He was obviously demanding their business, because one of her keepers immediately launched into some kind of explanation, gesturing towards her and smiling. She heard the name 'Paulus' several times until the guard finally nodded and allowed them to pass, holding open the tent flap as she was pushed inside.

She stood rubbing her wrists to bring the blood flow back into them while the two men gazed around. 'Look at this lot! All the bleeding comforts of home, and there's you and me lying on the cold hard ground while this bastard lives it up in the lap of luxury. I wouldn't mind a bit of this meself.'

'Forget it; you ain't a prefect, or a patrician with a rich daddy in Rome. Let's face it, you and me are just battle fodder, mate. Best we can hope for is to survive long enough to retire to a nice little farm somewhere.' He smiled with anticipation. 'Me? I'm going to get me one of them pretty little Gaul girls with a chest like a pouter pigeon and a good pair of childbearing hips, settle down, and make wine and babies.'

'No ambition,' his tall friend sneered. 'By the time I'm finished, I'm going to be a bleeding centurion. You just watch me.'

'Not if you don't do what you're bloody told. If Paulus comes back and finds us still hanging around, we'll be on latrine duty for the next six months. Get on with it, and let's get out of here. I'm starving. My stomach thinks my throat's been cut.'

'Right, bitch, time to put you back on your leash.' Grabbing Branna's arms, the guard bound her wrists firmly behind her back with a length of leather. 'There, that should keep you out of trouble.' He ran his hands over her exposed breasts, pinching her nipples viciously. When they hardened beneath his touch he bent over and ran his tongue over them. She shuddered in disgust, and he grinned at her. 'Just getting you in the mood for when Paulus comes back,' he leered. 'He'll be wanting to sample your charms, no doubt about that. He'll want to see if Iceni whores are any different from the ones in Rome.'

'Leave it,' his companion tugged impatiently on his sleeve, 'and let's get out of here. After we've eaten I've got a skin of wine tucked away, and I want a chance to win back that money you took off me the other night.'

'You'll be lucky, as I'm the best dice player in the legion. You might as well hand over the rest of your pay right now - it'll save you the bother of doing it later.' He chuckled to himself.

Branna sighed with relief as they headed back towards the entrance of the tent, and then left her there alone with no idea what she was in store for. She stood motionless in the centre of the luxuriously appointed space listening until the sound of their voices died away. Then, satisfied they would not return, she looked around her. The first thing she had to do was free herself, but a cursory inspection revealed nothing she could use to cut her bonds. Her eyes lingered on an empty wine amphora lying near the entrance. If she broke it she could use one of the shards to saw through the leather around her wrists.

Crouching awkwardly, she fumbled behind her until she could get a grip on the vessel, and pick it up. Then she backed towards the central tent pole and swung the amphora against it. There was a dull thudding down, but the vessel remained intact. Cursing softly she tried again and this time it shattered, leaving her holding one of the handles. She held her breath, waiting for the guard at the entrance to come bursting in and demand to know what she was doing. When the tent flap remained undisturbed, she let out a sigh of relief.

Kneeling down she dropped the handle, scrabbled behind her, and closed her fingers around the biggest shard, cutting them in the process. She winced, but at least she knew it was sharp. Then easing herself into a more comfortable position, she pulled her wrists apart until the leather was stretched taut between them, twisted her hand until the edge of the shard came into contact with it, and began to saw.

The task was more difficult than she had thought it would be. The leather was wet, the sharp edge of the clay slipped off it, and her fingers were both slippery and sticky with blood. Twice she dropped the fragment and had to fumble to find it again. Her hands were becoming numb from the pressure around her wrists, and her shoulder muscles ached from the strain. The temptation to simply give up was overwhelming, but she persevered, panting with the effort of keeping up a regular rhythm.

Finally she felt the first tiny give as the leather began to fray. She redoubled her efforts, and within minutes her bonds snapped, and she was free. She brought her hands around in front of her and began massaging her wrists, groaning in pain as the blood rushed back into her fingers. Her first overpowering instinct was to try and escape, but she dismissed it. Even if she somehow managed to get past the guard - a highly unlikely prospect - she would still be in the middle of the enemy camp, and she had no illusions as to her fate if she fell into the hands of the common soldiers. They would fall on her like wolves, and she shuddered at the thought of their hands ripping the clothes from her body. No, she would have to be more cunning than that.

Her mind raced as she tried to see a way out, discarding one wild idea after another. This was a temporary camp. The rebellion was over now, which meant they would soon be moving back to their permanent quarters, and once they were actually on the march there would be more opportunities for her to get away. They could not watch her all the time.

Meanwhile, she would have to fend for herself as best she could.

She stood up and looked around again, taking her surroundings in properly for the first time. And what surroundings they were. Despite the fact that this was only a tent, it was bigger and more luxurious than any place she had ever seen in her short life. The inside of the canvas was lined with a gleaming material she had never seen before, and stepping towards it, she ran her unstained hand over it, marvelling at its softness.

Thunder growled outside and a cold wind began to rise, making the tent billow as the first heavy raindrops spattered against it, but a charcoal brazier standing on a tripod near the central pole radiated a comfortable warmth. Oil lamps hung from chains, and by their light she could make out a low divan scattered with bright cushions, its ends curved and gilded, resting on a dais. Her eyes widened in wonder; whoever owned all this must be rich beyond imagining.

Her stomach grumbled, reminding her it had been a long time since she had last eaten. Beside the divan stood a small round table strewn with the remains of a meal. Offering up thanks to the gods, Branna crossed the tent towards it, almost stumbling in her eagerness. There was not much left, just a hunk of dry bread, a bone with a few shreds of meat still clinging to it, a fragment of cheese, and a small pottery bowl half-filled with round green and black seeds she did not recognise - yet for her the meagre repast was a feast.

The bread was hard as stone but had been smeared with honey, and she sat on the edge of the divan chewing it hungrily while savouring the fleeting sweetness. Licking her fingers for the last traces of goodness, she picked up the bone and gnawed on it, tearing the flecks of meat off before cracking it to get at the marrow, and suck it dry. She ate the cheese just as quickly, and then poked the contents of the bowl doubtfully, but hunger drove her on. She picked up one of the soft green seeds and nibbled it gingerly. It tasted oily and bitter but it was somehow satisfying, so she devoured them all, spitting the small black stones of their cores back into the bowl.

Two earthenware jugs stood beside the table. One was half-filled with water and the other contained a little of something else. She sniffed it suspiciously, and recognised the heavy sour-sweet smell of wine. She poured the mixture into a metal goblet, and immediately she could tell it was of far better quality than the wine her captors had given her. She drank it greedily, feeling its warmth spreading through her tired body.

The moment she finished eating and drinking her head began to nod, and she had to jerk herself upright again. She could not permit herself the indulgence of sleep. The owner of the tent and all its marvels must be due back soon. She got up and crossed the floor, picked up the shard of pottery she had used to saw through her bonds, and returned to the divan to wait, her mouth set in a determined line. She ran her finger over the sharp edge of the clay, and smiled. It had severed her bonds and would sever a throat equally well, if need be.

'Wait for me, Cerdoc, my beloved,' she whispered. 'I shall join you in the next world soon enough.'

When she awoke, Branna found herself lying against silk cushions. The oil lamps were flickering low, and she stared into the shadows cursing herself for her weakness. The tent was empty, but something must have disturbed her. She strained her ears... and heard the murmur of voices outside.

Slowly, she sat up, fumbling for her makeshift weapon and clenching it in her fist like a dagger as she hardly dared to breathe. The tent flap parted, and a tall figure appeared in the entrance. She raised her arm, lurched to her feet, and flung herself towards it, screaming the battle cry of her tribe and exulting as she dealt a killing blow straight to the heart...

Her crude weapon glanced harmlessly off body armour and she staggered back, staring in dismayed bewilderment at the useless shard of clay in her hand. Then a thudding blow to her cheek sent her reeling, and she would have fallen if strong hands had not gripped her arms and held her upright. Her heart racing, she stared up into the face of the man holding her prisoner. It was a handsome face at first glance, lean-jawed, with high cheekbones and chiselled features, but then she looked closer, and shivered. The lips were wet and petulant, and the eyes... Toutatis save her from the look in those eyes. Once, when she was a girl, she found a toad squatting on a stone beside the river, and it had looked at her with eyes very much like these; black and soulless and utterly alien. Then the man smiled down at her, and she shuddered again.

'So, the little Iceni bitch has teeth.' His voice was soft and cultured, but beneath the gentleness was a sinister layer of amused cruelty. His fingers dug deeper into her soft skin, forcing her to bite back a whimper of pain. 'And what do we do with a she-dog that bites?' he mused. 'Why, we beat her until she learns never to do it again.' His smile deepened. 'So it's time for your lesson, bitch.'

She did not understood a word he said, but she read his expression clearly enough and began to struggle frantically in his grasp, her fingernails sliding uselessly off his armour as she clawed at him. She kicked at his legs, wincing as her feet connected with the metal of his shin-guards. But her struggles merely served to amuse him.

Letting go of her arm, he wrenched the remnants of her tunic from her upper body, exposing her heaving breasts. He fondled them roughly, and pinched her nipples so hard she had to suppress a scream. His excitement mounting, he tore her skirt away, savouring the sight of her narrow waist and the full swell of her hips as the dim light gleamed on her soft white skin. Grinning wolfishly, he dragged her naked and writhing across the tent and flung her facedown over the end of the divan, exposing her plump young buttocks to his gloating gaze. She gasped, the breath knocked from her lungs as the couch's carved wooden end dug into her tender belly. Effectively paralysed, she glanced over her shoulder and saw him reaching for his belt, from which he pulled a short leather quirt he flexed between his hands.

Then he raised his arm, and brought it down with all his might across her cheeks. The tender flesh of her bottom jerked and quivered beneath the vicious blow, and a thin white line appeared across her skin, which quickly turned scarlet as the blood rushed back into it. She arched her back and her mouth opened in a silent scream of agony. But even worse than the unbelievable pain was the sound of her tormentor's high-pitched giggle as he raised his arm once more, and the quirt whistled through the air again.

The second blow was even worse than the first as the weapon cut its way into her already tender flesh, and as a third and fourth welt criss-crossed the first two, she felt as though burning brands were being laid across the soft globes of her buttocks. Finally she found her voice and a tortured shriek escaped her lips as she glanced over her shoulder again. Apparently the sound of her pain and the sight of her wriggling bottom inflamed him, for she saw him reach beneath his leather kilt to fondle himself.

'Go on, bitch, *beg*.' He leaned over to trace the pattern of weals on her skin with the end of the quirt.

The slight touch sent more pain searing through her, but she bit her lip, determined not to give him the satisfaction of hearing her cry out again, which proved a mistake.

'Not learned your lesson yet?' He raised his arm again.

The flurry of blows that followed reduced her to a writhing mass of pure agony. Gasps and sobs and whimpers and pleas filled her ears, and yet she was scarcely aware of the fact that they were issuing from her own throat. By the time he finally stopped beating her, she had not only forgotten her vow not to cry out, but she had completely forgotten her pride and everything but the pain consuming her... or almost everything. To her utter horror she became aware of a very different sort of heat spreading through her lower belly. Her nipples were stiff and grazing against the silk divan in a highly stimulating away, and she shuddered, her humiliation complete, when she felt the aroused moisture between her thighs.

She stiffened, desperately trying to resist the excitement spreading through her. She looked back again, and saw her tormentor panting from the effort of beating her, and with lust, his *membrum virilis* jutting out from beneath his leather kilt stiff as an iron rod. She could feel that her bottom was a fiery red as he dropped the quirt and reached down to knead her smouldering cheeks, clearly savouring the way she winced and trembled beneath his touch. Smiling, he ran a finger down the cleft of her buttocks until he found the hot and aching centre of her body. He parted the delicate lips of her labia, and she gasped as he exposed the glistening pink flesh within. Then she groaned as he thrust two fingers up inside her and began sliding them in and out of her silky depths.

'So, the little bitch is in heat now.' He withdrew his fingers and rubbed his cock until it was slippery with her juices, then he pushed the head against her cleft, slowly rubbing it up and down.

Branna thought she would go mad from a tormenting mix of pain and pleasure. She whimpered as she fought the urge to impale herself on his cock, and satisfy the vile lust coursing through her. She shuddered with relief as he pulled back again, but it was only to pull apart the cheeks of her bottom, and she caught her breath in horror as she felt his swollen glans pushing against the reluctantly puckered entrance to her anus. Her gasp became a cry of pain as he continued to force himself into her. There was a brief flare of agony, then her sphincter's resistance melted and his erection slid smoothly inside, filling her to the hilt. He remained motionless for a moment before he began moving swiftly in and out of her bottom, grunting with delight at the tightness gripping him.

She gritted her teeth, bracing herself against the torment, and the wicked tendrils of pleasure it was perversely causing to bloom inside her. *By all the gods, this Roman was conquering her in the most terrible way imaginable, by showing her she was as perverted as he was!*

Against her will, her hand strayed down between her thighs and she began fingering herself as he thrust and snorted like a rutting boar behind her. His strokes became faster and more furious, and her fingers matched them as they slid in and out of her soaking pussy. She groaned and pushed back against him, forcing him even deeper into her body's forbidden depths. Then, suddenly, she felt his cock jerk and shudder, his hot milk erupted into her, and the exquisite sensation triggered her own breathtaking release.

After a moment he pulled out of her and she collapsed against the divan, sobbing with shame and humiliation as the seed of her mortal enemy trickled down the insides of her thighs. She had betrayed both her lover and her people. Death would have been better, and much cleaner, than this.

'Stop your whimpering,' he snapped, 'and get up. I'm hungry.'

As she rose stiffly to her feet he stalked across to the tent flap, stuck his head out, and yelled a command. A few minutes later a soldier hurried into the tent carrying a tray he placed deferentially on the table beside the divan. Then he saluted and departed, but not before casting an envious glance at Branna as he did so.

Divesting himself of his armour, the prefect reclined across the divan and waved a lordly hand her way. 'Serve me,' he said, indicating she should pour his wine first. She bent to pick up her discarded tunic, but he reached across and tore the cloth from her nerveless fingers. 'Oh no you don't,' he snapped. 'I've a mind to emulate our dear emperor, Nero; being waited on by a naked slave will make my meal so much more enjoyable.'

So as she stood watching him eat, Branna's stomach churned hungrily again at the sight of fresh meat and soft bread. There was fruit, too, and cheese. Her mouth watered even as she smiled bitterly to herself; she might wish to die, but she would prefer to do it on a full stomach.

At last the Roman swallowed his last mouthful, wiped his hands fastidiously, and smiled at her. 'You must be hungry, too,' he said in a purring voice, and indicated the remains of his meal with a gracious nod of his head.

She approached the table warily.

Quick as a snake striking, he grabbed her arm and yanked her down to her knees before him. 'If you're hungry,' he said quietly, 'I've got just the thing for you.' He lifted his tunic to reveal his cock, which was eager and ready again. 'Eat *this*, my dear.'

She struggled to pull away, but he transferred his grip to her long braid and pulled her face towards his groin. One of her flailing hands hit the small table, knocking it over, and her fingers suddenly found the short dagger he had used to carve his meat. She snatched it up, there was a scream, and she was free. She staggered to her feet, dropping the knife as she did so, and backed away from him. His hands were covering his face and she saw blood trickling between his fingers. She grinned savagely. She had cut him from temple to jaw. When the wound healed he would not be quite so pretty. His twisted face would match his twisted soul.

'Guard!' he shrieked. 'Guard!'

The soldier came running into the tent, and then stopped dead, glancing back and forth from his superior's bloody countenance to Branna's lovely face as comprehension dawned. 'Yes, sir?' he asked at last.

'Send for the camp physician at once! And as for this... this *she-wolf*, give her to the men. They can do whatever they like with her!' He smiled venomously as blood dripped from his chin. 'And if she's not dead by the time they've finished with her, then kill her yourself.'

As the soldier approached her cautiously Branna backed away from him, her eyes darting around the tent for something to defend herself with. The prefect's discarded armour still lay where he had dropped it, and she promptly snatched up the short-sword and sank into a crouch, holding it out before her.

The man stopped well out of its reach, uncertain what to do next.

'Don't just stand there staring like an idiot!' his superior yelled. 'She's only a slip of a girl, take her!'

'Shall I kill her, sir?'

'And ruin my Turkish carpets, are you mad? No, I want her taken alive. I want her to suffer for what she's done to me. If you can't do the job, then find someone who can.'

The soldier promptly walked back to the entrance, and shouted to someone outside. Within seconds the flap burst open and a burly figure strode into the tent, followed by two more men. One of them was the centurion who had dragged Maximus off her in the clearing. Without a word, he strode towards the sword weaving dangerously in Branna's hand. He stopped just beyond its reach, pulled off his cloak, whirled it around, and flung it at her. The thick wool settled over her like a net, and nearly suffocated her in its wet folds as she thrust out blindly, but the blade was also hopelessly entangled. As she struggled to release it stout arms wrapped around her, pinning her own arms to her sides. The weapon fell to the floor, and she was flung kicking and screaming over someone's shoulder.

'What shall I do with the prisoner now, sir?' the centurion asked calmly as she writhed against him, sobbing with fury.

'Do I have to repeat myself forever? Take her away and give her to the men. They can fuck her blind, just get her out of here.'

The centurion strode out of the tent, and Branna felt the cold rain soaking through the cloak and running off her bare legs as she was carried through the camp. Then she was thrown down on the ground on her excruciatingly tender bottom, and the wet cloak was ripped off her. She was inside another tent, only this one was so small the three men had to stoop to enter it, and there was barely room for all of them. All their eyes were on her naked body, and the only thing she had to cover herself with were her arms.

'Let's draw lots to see who goes first,' one of the soldiers suggested eagerly. 'I want her while she's still fresh.'

'Nobody's having her,' the centurion said firmly. 'That bastard took her away from me once, but he's not doing it again. If he wasn't man enough to keep her, that's his problem. She's mine now.'

'But what about his orders? He said she was to be given to the men. He won't be too pleased when he finds out you disobeyed him.'

'Oh yes? And just who is going to tell him... *you?*' He smiled menacingly. 'Soldiering is a dangerous job, boy. How would you like to find yourself on the front line in our next skirmish?'

'No, sir, I won't tell him,' the younger man muttered, diligently examining his boots.

'Good.' The centurion's smile became more pleasant. 'I'm glad we've got that little matter sorted out.' He rummaged in the pouch at his belt, and handed the soldier a few coins. 'There, treat yourself to a skin of wine and a couple of whores when we get back to barracks.'

16

'Thank you, sir, that's very generous of you, sir.'

The centurion's smile vanished again. 'Just remember,' he said quietly, 'not a word to anyone. Not if you value that pathetic hide of yours.'

The man backed out of the tent, and his companions followed him reluctantly, their eyes lingering hungrily on Branna. Once they were alone the centurion stared calculatingly down at her, and she stared helplessly back at him. She was cold and wet and frightened; all her fight had gone. He could do whatever he liked with her. She did not have the strength to resist him. When he leaned over her, she cringed.

'No need to look like that, girl,' he spoke haltingly in her own tongue. 'You're safe enough with me. I prefer the nice tight buttocks of a boy, myself.'

She looked up at him in astonishment, and then shrugged philosophically. As long as he did not intend to ravish her, she did not care what perversions he practiced.

'You wish to eat?' he asked her.

She nodded eagerly, and watched in delicious anticipation as he rummaged through a leather satchel and produced some bread and cheese. She literally snatched the cheese from his hand, and thrust the semi-hard hunk ravenously into her mouth. She was so engrossed in the food she did not notice as he turned away from her and poured some wine into a cup. He handed it to her, and she drank it down greedily. She had barely finished eating when a wave of dizziness washed over her, and suddenly all her limbs felt leaden. She stared at him, her pupils dilating in horror as she realised he had poisoned her. This was the last dreadful thought that flickered through her mind before her consciousness spiralled away into darkness.

CHAPTER 2

When Branna opened her eyes all she could still see was darkness, and after a moment she became aware of the fact that she was wrapped up in a coarse cloth. Panic gripped her. *She was buried alive!*

Her chest heaved as she gasped for air in the suffocating blackness of the grave, struggling frantically against the weight of her shroud. But it was useless; there was no escape from death. Terror overwhelmed her, and she ceased to struggle.

Gradually it dawned on her that she was being bumped and jolted, and commonsense reasserted itself; graves did not move, nor were they so noisy, of that she was sure.

Straining her ears, she could make out muffled sounds penetrating the thick cloth in which she was wrapped. She was hearing marching feet and the clink of armour, the creaking of wagon wheels, and mules and horses snorting. Her fingers explored the material covering her. It felt vaguely familiar, and finally she pieced together that she was on a baggage train bound and wrapped in the folds of a tent. Her mouth was dry and tasted foul, and her head pounded dully, but she ignored these sensations as she tested her bonds. Her ankles were tied tightly together, but a slightly longer rope linked her wrists, allowing her hands some freedom of movement. She clawed at the knots in an attempt to undo them, but her fingernails broke uselessly against the thick hemp, and she closed her eyes again in despair.

It seemed an eternity before the constant jolting finally ceased. She heard men laughing and calling to each other, and she managed not to cry out in alarm as the surface she lay on was tugged away, causing the tent she was wrapped in to roll down to the wooden floor of the baggage cart.

'What about this one of Gaius's?' a voice inquired.

She held her breath, expecting to be discovered at any moment.

'Leave it,' answered another voice. 'He didn't give any orders, did he? The bugger can fetch it for himself.'

The voices receded, and she began to breathe easily again. She lay there for what felt like hours, and was beginning to think she would lie there forever when her sharp ears caught the sound of soft footsteps. Then she felt hands fumbling at the canvas covering her, and suddenly she was breathing fresh air. After so much time spent in absolute darkness, even the dim twilight made her blink like a startled owl.

When her eyes adjusted she discerned the face of the centurion she believed had poisoned her. The men had called him 'Gaius'. He helped her to her feet, and wrapped his cloak around her naked body. She stumbled and would have fallen if he had not caught her against him, and then led her to a small grove of trees, where he allowed her to tend to her bodily needs before leading her back to the wagon, where he handed her a skin of water and a package of food.

'Stay put,' he ordered gruffly in her language. 'And you can forget about trying to escape.' His eyes crawled over her, and he smiled grimly. 'The men haven't had a woman in weeks. If they caught you, even I wouldn't be able to stop them having their disgusting way with you.'

She understood all too well. Cowering down, she allowed him to pull the thick canvas over her again, sealing her back in darkness.

Hour followed weary hour as the legion marched back to its barracks. Bound as much by fear as by the ropes around her wrists, Branna lay in her hiding place with nothing but her thoughts for company. At the end of each day Gaius returned to bring her a few moments of freedom - a tantalising glimpse of sky and a few glorious breaths of fresh air. Even the howling wind and the cold rain beating against her exposed skin was a pleasure after being cooped up for so long. But these moments were all too brief, and then she was returned to her claustrophobic prison.

At long last the monotony was broken by an unusual occurrence. The cart containing the tents rumbled to a halt, Branna heard voices, and then it began to move again, but more slowly. After another stretch of time the wagon stopped again, this time for good. She waited for Gaius to come.

And waited.

And waited.

Panic began to well up inside her. Her water jar was empty, she had long since eaten her meagre supply of food, and she was desperate to empty her bowels and her bladder. Whimpering, she clenched her muscles against the ultimate humiliation of soiling herself. Then finally the canvas covering was dragged roughly away and she staggered up. Unable to contain herself another second, she squatted beside the back wheel of the cart and relieved herself like an animal. When she was finished, she wiped herself with a handful of leaves and stood up with as much dignity as she could muster, looking around her.

The baggage cart stood on a hillside clearing overlooking other open fields. She saw more tethered horses than she had ever seen before in her life, and beyond them she glimpsed a huge city of tents and wooden buildings. The original camp was a paltry affair compared to this one. 'W-where are we?' she breathed. 'What is this place?'

'Dubris barracks,' Gaius informed her.

As her eyes adjusted to the dim twilight, she could make out the lines of a stockade in the distance topped by the tiny silhouettes of figures holding spears, and for the first time she was struck by the foolhardiness of her tribe in attempting to defeat the might of such an empire as this.

Gaius interrupted her thoughts. 'Here,' he muttered. He untied one of her wrists, and then rummaged through a leather satchel and produced a soft bundle. 'Put these on.'

She caught the bundle of clothing, and shook it out. There was a short woollen tunic and a dark cloak, threadbare but still serviceable. For a moment she wondered whom they had originally belonged to and what had become of their owner.

'Don't just stand there,' he said testily. 'We haven't got all night.' He let the rope go long enough for her to slip the tunic on over her head, but then seized it again. She shivered as the rough wool irritated her tender skin. Picking up the cloak he wrapped it around her, and then in a gesture that reminded her painfully of her mother, he tugged the hood up to hide the tangled mass of her golden hair. Finally, he reached into the satchel again and withdrew a pair of battered sandals. They were far too big for her, but she wound the thongs around her calves and knotted them firmly to hold them in place. 'Good,' he muttered, looking her up and down. Then he yanked on the rope and forced her to follow behind him like a recalcitrant dog.

She dug her heels in, and he turned and glared at her.

'W-where do we go?' she asked haltingly, in his language.

He raised an eyebrow. 'So, you know more than you let on, do you?' he said. 'Excellent. That should raise your price a bit. As for where we're going, you'll find that out soon enough. Come on, and keep your head down.' He turned and strode off, and she had no choice but to stumble along behind him.

Her head bowed, she followed him through the camp, fear of discovery making her stick as close to him as possible. But apart from the occasional greeting, to which Gaius replied with a brusque nod of his head, no one paid them much attention.

After a few muttered words to the guards at the gate, they left the barracks and made their way down through the town, and for the first time she noticed the tang of salt in the air. The smells became stronger and the winding streets dirtier and meaner the farther they walked, and occasionally women's voices would call out coaxingly, and colourfully clad figures would beckon enticingly from the shadows. Branna shrank away from them. She had heard of the brazen women who made their living selling their bodies to all comers, but this was the first time she had ever actually seen them.

At last they turned down a dockside alley and halted in front of a dilapidated wine shop. As Gaius pushed open the door the sound of coarse voices and the high screech of drunken female laughter spilled out onto the street. He dragged her in after him, but she paused on the threshold, blinking against the dim light. She had never seen anything like this place. Seamen of every creed and colour seemed to be doing their best to spend their pay as fast as possible, and the women were all too eager to help them.

In one dark corner a girl with scarlet lips sat on one man's knee while another man suckled at her naked breasts. Her legs were parted, and both men's hands were working between her thighs. Branna blushed and looked away, but the girl caught her expression, and a scowl crossed her face as she pushed the men away and staggered to her feet. 'What the fuck do you think you're staring at?' the whore demanded, glaring at Branna, but when Gaius gave her a contemptuous glance her indignation mysteriously dissolved, and she turned her attention back to her suitors.

Gaius wound his way between the wine-stained tables, tugging Branna along behind him. The men cast surreptitious glances at the couple, and then quickly averted their eyes. Clearly, in places like this it did not pay to take too much interest in other peoples' business. The women stared at them a little longer, eyeing Gaius speculatively, before they, too, seemingly lost interest.

When they reached the darkest corner of the bar, a small round figure in flowing robes got to his feet and bowed to them. Branna's nose wrinkled beneath the wave of perfumed oil that wafted her way, but which did little to mask the smell of unwashed flesh.

'Gaius, my friend,' the man murmured, rubbing his hands together. 'Some wine before business?'

Gaius nodded, and sat down opposite the rotund figure, leaving Branna standing beside him.

Their host clicked his fingers, and the keeper of the wine shop immediately hurried over to them with an amphora.

Once the wine was poured the two men raised their cups to each other. 'You are well, Gaius?' the stranger inquired politely.

'Well enough, Habib,' the Roman answered. 'And you?'

'Business is bad,' Habib sighed dramatically, 'as always.' He shook his head sadly. 'The risks are high and the prices low, but what is a poor man to do?'

'A poor man!' Gaius laughed mirthlessly. 'You could buy and sell the lot of us.' His eyes narrowed. 'Don't try and plead poverty to me, Habib. If you don't want to buy, there are plenty who do.' He made as if to rise.

Habib tugged him back down again. 'Did I say that?' he demanded in an injured tone. 'Come now, Gaius, do not be so hasty. Let us see what kind of merchandise you are offering first.'

Gaius pulled the cloak away from Branna's face, and her long hair tumbled down over her shoulders. Then, before she could stop him, he stood up and tugged both the cloak and her tunic up to reveal her naked body.

Habib's eyes widened in appreciation.

Branna cringed, but forced herself to hold still as the merchant ran his greasy hands over her, enjoying the smooth firmness of her flesh. He pinched her nipples, and then cupped her breasts in the palms of his hands, weighing them as if they were ripe fruits, and she closed her eyes as he completed his inspection by slipping his fingers between her thighs to examine her vulva. Then, thankfully, Gaius covered her again.

'Nice,' Habib murmured. 'Very nice,' he repeated, and promptly named a sum.

Gaius shook his head. 'Do you take me for a fool?' he scoffed. 'I could get twice as much as that.'

The haggling continued for another five minutes or so, until both men were satisfied. A fat purse then exchanged hands, and they sealed the deal with another drink before Gaius got to his feet again.

Branna grabbed his arm in a panic. 'You cannot leave me with this man!' she gasped.

He shrugged off her hand. 'You're no longer my concern,' he told her indifferently. 'You belong to him now.'

She stared after him as he wended his way out of the place without another glance back at her, and then she turned and stared fearfully at Habib, her new master. Bitterness washed through her as the reality of her slavery sank in. She was no longer a person; she was nothing but a piece of meat. Habib swilled down more wine, smacked his thick lips, and ran his eyes over her again, a smirk of satisfaction on his face. Then his expression became ruthlessly calculating as he studied her more closely. The rope Gaius had used to bind her still hung from her wrists, and picking up the trailing end, he used it as a makeshift whip to suddenly administer several sharp blows to her hips.

Branna gasped in shock and her eyes filled with tears as the rope curled around her, stinging her tender bottom even through the woollen tunic. Her humiliation was made even worse by laughter and jeers from the tavern's rowdy patrons, who regarded the scene of her indignity as just one small part of the evening's entertainment.

Then Habib stood up, gave her an uncompromising shove, and she stumbled reluctantly towards the door. Once they were out in the street she took deep, grateful breaths of the cool night air. It was a blessed relief after the hot and smoky atmosphere of the bar, and she savoured it for as long as possible before another lash from the rope startled her into moving again. The smell of the sea grew heavier the farther they walked, until finally the dark and winding alley opened out onto a dock. She stopped short, and stared around with her mouth open in wonder.

Several ships rode at anchor and loomed above her like strange sea-monsters. They moved restlessly on the waves, and she could hear low creaking and grinding noises as if they were groaning in their sleep. Her nose tickled, and she sneezed as she was assaulted by a host of scents - the aroma of exotic spices, the smell of pitch, and the stench of bilges. And above it all the stars glittered with an icy, merciless brightness. She was tempted to run to the edge of the dock and fling herself into the sea, and as if sensing her feelings, Habib tugged her even more quickly and firmly along behind him. They passed two great ships towering above the rest, several sturdy boats with leather sails, and a cluster of small fishing craft, before her new owner finally came to a stop.

Branna looked around her again. Living in the hills, the sea had been nothing but a distant gleaming line on the horizon when one climbed high enough to catch a glimpse of it. The only crafts she had ever seen before tonight were the occasional riverboats that brought traders to the *oppida*. Even so, there was something about the vessel before which they stood that struck her. Although it was apparently built to carry a substantial cargo, its lines still gave the impression of great speed.

Habib took her stunned silence for admiration. 'Made to my own specifications by the best shipbuilder on the Mediterranean,' he informed her. 'Capable of carrying more than fifty slaves and still outrunning any pirate ship on the sea.'

She glanced at him. Although she could not understand what he was saying, she could sense his pride and her lip curled in disdain. 'What a brave warrior you are,' she retorted in her own language. 'It must take real courage to capture helpless women and children. Oh, but I forgot, you don't capture them, do you? You simply buy them from those who do, like rats that eat the grain others have harvested.' She spat at his feet. 'May you die squealing in the gutter like the filthy vermin you are!'

Her words meant nothing to him, but her tone stung him to the quick. He looked up from the spittle spattering his sandals to the expression of disdain on her face. He raised his hand as if to strike her, but the exultant smile on her face stopped him when he seemed to realise this was what she wanted.

'Oh no, my pretty one,' he said quietly, lowering his hand, 'there are far more profitable ways of wiping that smile from your lips than bruising that lovely face. We'll see how much fight is left in you after a few days in the hold.' He yanked on her rope so viciously that she nearly fell at his feet. 'Now come, we are going aboard. I have wasted enough time standing here.'

When they reached the bottom of the gangplank, she shied away like a startled horse. The narrow piece of wood swayed alarmingly with the movement of the ship, and cold terror gripped her. One slip and she would fall into the icy water and be crushed between the ship and the dock. She shuddered; death might be a release, but not such a horrible death as being ground to a bloody pulp.

Ignoring her whimpers of terror, Habib hauled her up the gangplank like a mule on a halter. It trembled beneath her feet but thankfully did not give way, and when they reached the top, he let go of her rope and allowed her to collapse into a quivering heap at his feet.

'Not so brave now, are you, my little warrior maiden?' He stirred her with the toe of his sandal, chuckling.

She glared up at him with one last spark of defiance, and attempted to spit at him again, but her mouth was too dry with fear. And he was not looking at her anyway as he clapped his hands and called out imperiously.

A wiry old man and a dark-skinned boy appeared as if from nowhere, and waited expectantly.

'You, take her below with the others,' Habib commanded, pointing to the old man. Then he turned his attention to the boy. 'And you, inform the ship's cook that I am back and will take supper in my cabin immediately.'

While her new master feasted in the comfort of his cabin, Branna was led away to much less pleasant quarters. The old man herded her along the deck to a hatch in the stern of the ship, muttering and cursing beneath his breath as he bent over to haul it open.

She wrinkled her nose in distaste as a gust of stale air assaulted her nostrils, then she stared down in dismay at the yawning darkness. It was like looking at the entrance to the underworld, and she could even hear the low moaning sound of lost souls rising from below. She backed as far away from the hatch as the rope around her would permit.

'Get back here!' the old man snarled, tugging on her leash. 'The sooner I gets yer down there with the rest of 'em, the sooner I gets me supper.' Seizing her by the arm, he pushed her towards the dark hole. She teetered on the edge, and for one horrifying moment thought she would tumble down into the pit, but instead she fell forward onto the deck, half in and half out of the hold. Then her feet found the rungs of a wooden ladder and she began the awkward descent, gripping the struts as best she could with her bound hands. The old man followed her as nimbly as a monkey, and she was forced to move more quickly so he would not tread on her fingers. At the bottom she stopped and looked around her in despair.

A single oil lamp hung from a chain, and by its flickering light she could see a little way into the belly of the ship. The scene reminded her of the byres where cattle were kept in winter, only here the cattle was human. The ribs of the ship divided the space into small compartments, and each one contained three to four people. Dirty straw covered the deck, and the stench of unwashed humanity was appalling.

At the sound of their entrance a few of the prisoners raised their heads, stared at Branna with dull eyes for a moment, and then looked away. Some were so engrossed in their own misery that they failed to notice her arrival completely. The moaning was louder now that she was in the hold, a constant litany of woe made up of women sobbing and men groaning. There was another sound, too, one Branna did not recognise, until the old man untied her and hauled her towards the nearest stall. He rummaged in the filthy straw, produced a set of manacles, and clipped them around her wrists and ankles. She recognised the sound then - the slow, metallic susurration of chain-links sliding over each other in response to the restless movement of prisoners.

The old man made sure her shackles were secure, then wiped his hands on his filthy tunic and headed back towards the ladder, and his overdue supper. Climbing up as nimbly as he had clambered down, he slammed the hatch closed behind him, cutting off Branna's last frail hope of escape.

Claustrophobia began setting in as the walls of the ship closed in around her, and her lungs laboured to draw in the nauseous, stale air. Her breathing became ragged and dizziness blurred her vision. Staggering backwards, she collided with the rough wood of the hull and slid down into a sitting position. Her terror was so great that when a hand was laid gently on her shoulder she almost shrieked aloud. But stifling her cry, she looked up into a pair of sympathetic brown eyes belonging to a girl roughly her own age.

'I am no enemy,' the other slave assured her. 'I am Tallis of the Trinovantes, and you are safe now with me.' She spoke soothingly in Branna's own tongue. 'Breathe deeply and slowly... that's it...' she coaxed, 'that's it.'

Branna took one last shuddering breath and forced herself to smile up at her comforter. 'Thank you,' she said gratefully. 'I am Branna of the Iceni, and I ask your pardon. My cowardice shames both me and my tribe.'

'Hah! I wouldn't let that worry you,' her new companion retorted. 'You're not the only one. I've seen grown men weep when the chains were put on them.'

'H-how long have you been here?'

Tallis shrugged. 'Who knows, time means nothing down here, but the moon was full when they first brought me to the ship.'

Branna gaped at her, her pupils dilating in horror, for the moon was almost full again now. 'How can you bear it?' she gasped.

The girl lifted her manacled wrists, and shook them. 'Does it look as if I had a choice?' she demanded. 'And at least I am still alive. The rest of my family was slaughtered.'

'As was my betrothed,' Branna declared bitterly. 'And I wish by Teutatis that I had died with him.'

'Well you didn't, so you might as well accept it,' Tallis stated bluntly. 'If dying was as easy as that, we would all be free.' She laughed humourlessly. 'I tried to starve myself at first, but by the third day I would have eaten raw horseflesh to still my gnawing belly.' Her eyes glinted in the semi-darkness like those of a feral cat. 'So I decided to live, and avenge my murdered family.'

'How?' Branna demanded bitterly. 'Shall we rise up and choke our captors with our chains? Or perhaps you have a dagger hidden in the straw?'

'Our time will come,' Tallis said with certainty. 'We will not always be in these chains.' Her lips drew back from her teeth in a snarl. 'And then we will repay our new masters in blood.'

Branna shivered; for a brief moment she saw madness flashing in the other girl's eyes. Much as she hated the Romans, she pitied whoever took Tallis as a slave; they would surely be safer clasping an adder to their chest.

Just then the sound of the hatch reopening drew their attention. 'Feeding time,' Tallis announced, her voice heavy with irony. 'Must keep the animals in good condition.'

Branna watched as two of the crew wrestled a heavy water barrel down the ladder, and rolled it into a corner. They then upended it, and began to dole the contents out to the chained prisoners. When it was her turn, Branna drank greedily.

Once everyone had been watered, the two crewmen left and returned a few moments later with food. It was poor stuff, only a hunk of stale bread and even harder cheese, but Branna devoured every last morsel, and then licked her fingers clean.

'Try and get some sleep now if you can,' Tallis advised. 'Nights are the worst, and at least in our dreams we still have our freedom.'

'Err... where do I...?' Branna's voice trailed away as she looked around for some private place to relieve herself.

'In the straw, where do you think? We're animals, remember? What's a little piss and shit to an animal?' Tallis pointed to a spot as far as possible from where they lay. 'Go there. That way, at least, we won't have to sleep in it, and just be grateful they change the straw occasionally.'

Grimacing, Branna did as she was told, pulling her chains as far as they would reach. She turned her back and squatted, and when she was finished she returned to her place and lay down, trying to get as comfortable as possible with the iron manacles digging into her flesh.

She lay awake for a long time, staring into the semi-darkness. The oil lamp had burned low and all she could see were the dim shadows of her fellow prisoners as they tossed and turned, moaning and whimpering. Occasionally she would catch the glint of eyes in the darkness, showing her that others were as restless as she. Finally, however, exhaustion and the gentle rocking of the ship lulled her into a restless sleep.

A hand on her shoulder brought her awake with a start. At first she thought it was Tallis, then her eyes opened and she found herself gazing into the leering face of the old man.

'Wakey wakey, sweetheart, you're in for a treat.' He bowed mockingly. 'The captain sends his compliments, and invites you to his cabin.' He unlocked her manacles, and pulled her to her feet with a strength that belied his age. 'Come on, hurry up,' he grumbled. 'The captain don't like to be kept waiting.' Dragging her behind him, he reached the foot of the ladder and pushed her towards it. 'Get up there, or it'll be the worse for you.'

Reluctantly she began to climb as slowly as possible, until a hand thrust between her thighs made her squeal and scramble to the top.

'Thought that'd shift yer,' the old man chuckled.

On deck, Branna looked wildly around her. If she ran for it perhaps she could fling herself over the ship's railing and swim to freedom.

'Oh no yer don't.' He quickly grabbed her wrist. 'Yer don't get away that easy.' Her feet slipping and sliding on the wet boards, he hauled her towards a cabin and knocked on the door. When Habib opened it he tugged on his forelock. 'The young lady you requested, sir.'

Habib nodded curtly, and the old man thrust her inside the room. The door banged closed behind her, and her new owner turned the key in the lock.

Branna stared at him, her chest heaving with fear and indignation. If he took so much as one step towards her, she would tear his throat out with her teeth.

He indicated a bowl of scented and steaming water on the table. 'Wash yourself,' he ordered, seating himself on a couch.

She looked from him to the hot water, seriously tempted by the desire to wash the stench from her body and be clean again, but she shook her head, stubbornly refusing to accept anything he offered her.

'You wash or I have you washed,' he said haltingly in her language, and then grinned, revealing stained brown teeth. 'Pretty girl you my men enjoy much.'

Branna shuddered at the thought, and gritting her teeth reached for the washcloth. She dipped it in the hot water, and gingerly dabbed her face and hands with it.

'No,' he snapped, 'you strip and wash all over.'

Pretending he was not there, she slipped the grimy and tatty tunic from her shoulders and allowed it to fall to her feet. Then she picked up the cloth again and began to wash herself properly, shivering at the feel of the cool water against her warm and filthy skin. As she scrubbed herself the water ran down her chest and belly in rivulets, sending little trickles of pleasure through her. She shivered again, and her nipples hardened. The flickering light from the oil lamp glistened off her wet body, outlining the swell of her hips, the pale globes of her breasts, and the sweet curve of her belly above her shadowy golden bush.

Smiling with satisfaction at his latest purchase, Habib reached for a pile of gossamer-thin purple garments and held them out towards her. 'You put on these,' he instructed.

Branna accepted the proffered material, shook it out, and gasped. It was so thin it was effectively transparent. She shook her head, and threw the shameful outfit at his feet.

'You wish I call two of my men to dress you?' he asked threateningly, picking the clothes up and thrusting them at her again.

Knowing it was hopeless to resist him, Branna dressed with trembling fingers, and then stood before him, her eyes closed in shame. The harem trousers billowed around her legs, and the small tight bodice clasped her breasts like a lover's hands, while every curve of her body was visible through the fine silk.

Still smiling, her owner moved to the cabin door, unlocked and opened it, and clapped his hands. The young dark-skinned boy appeared, this time clutching a small and bulbous brass instrument. 'Music,' Habib commanded him, and turned to Branna. 'And you dance for me.'

The boy scuttled across the cabin to sit cross-legged in a corner. Putting the instrument to his lips, he began to play a strange sinuous tune that seemed to coil its way through the hot air of the cabin like a living thing. Habib reclined on his divan, and put a strange implement in his mouth from which he drew an aromatic smoke. The scent made her head spin in an almost pleasant way, and as her eyelids drooped, she felt her body beginning to sway, her hips and shoulders undulating back and forth as the music insinuated itself into her blood. She kept her eyes half closed, but she could still see her master's gown had fallen open to reveal the hairy bulge of his belly. Beneath it his cock jutted out, the head thick and swollen as he watched her with a greedy expression on his plump face. She smiled distantly. It did not matter... nothing mattered... this was only a bad dream... a dream from which she would awake to find herself lying on a sunlit hillside wrapped in Cerdoc's arms...

The music grew faster and more insistent and perspiration trickled down her body, making the thin material of her outfit even more transparent as it clung to her like a second skin, outlining her nipples as they pressed against it. Excitement swelled inside her, imagining Cerdoc's mouth on hers, then his hands exploring her eager body, and her hips ground back and forth as the piping drove her into a strange sensual frenzy. Closing her eyes, she gave herself up to it completely and spread her legs so her fingers could stroke the moist cleft of her vulva and toy with the hard bud of her clitoris. Her lips parted and her breaths quickened as delicious sensations washed through her.

Then the music stopped abruptly.

She blinked, bewildered, as the dream vanished and left her rigidly awake in her living nightmare. The boy was gone and Habib was standing before her naked, his distended member pointing at her like an obscenely rigid snake. She attempted to back away from it, but he gripped her by the hair and pulled her towards him. She could feel his hard cock digging into her belly, and moaned in protest as his wet mouth came down on hers, his tongue squirming its way between her lips while his stubby fingers groped at her breasts and toyed with her sensitive nipples. Unable to move, Branna did the only thing she could do and bit down on his tongue, hard.

He released her so abruptly she nearly fell. He sank down on the edge of the divan, his hands covering his mouth. When he raised them there was blood on his fingers. He stared at it in disbelief, and then raised his furious eyes to hers. 'Bitch!' he muttered thickly. 'You'll pay for that.'

Quick as a panther despite his bulk, he was on his feet again before she knew it and ripping the delicate clothing from her body. Then he yanked her down over his knees, and his hand came down viciously across her naked bottom. She shrieked in humiliation and pain, struggling to free herself, but he held her firmly in place and raised his hand again. The soft flesh of her buttocks rolled and quivered as he spanked her, leaving his handprints on her delicate skin as she cried out and writhed beneath each blow. By the time he stopped her cheeks were a fiery scarlet, tears of pain and shame were coursing down her face, and his stiff cock was digging insistently into her belly. Reaching down he picked up the torn remnants of her harem trousers, twisted some of the material into a makeshift rope, and wrapped it around her wrists. Then he stood up, flipped her over onto her back across the divan, and secured the cloth to the raised edges of the gilded frame. She kicked wildly at him, but he caught her ankles and secured them as well. She now lay spread-eagled before him, completely helpless and vulnerable.

Gloating, Habib ran his hands all over her body, mauling her breasts and twisting her nipples between his thumb and forefinger until she cried out in distress. Then he straddled her, his heavy balls trailing against her ribs, his cock standing out rigid. He seized her breasts even harder, pushing them together and thrusting his erection between them, his thumbs playing with her nipples as he moved his hips back and forth. She turned her head away, avoiding the sight of his purple cockhead appearing and disappearing between her tender globes as he used them to pleasure himself.

Eventually tiring of masturbating himself with her breasts, he slid down her body, running his hands over her nipples and down her belly until he came to the downy hair leading into her most secret passage. Leering, he parted the lips of her vulva, and admired the soft glistening pinkness within. 'The gates of paradise,' he murmured.

Branna watched in disbelief as he lowered his head between her thighs, and then she felt his thick tongue lapping at her pussy. She squirmed, trying to escape his obscene attentions, but then he found the hard nub of her clitoris and she began to writhe again, this time in reluctant pleasure as he licked teasingly at the pearl of her flesh. Closing her eyes she tried to suppress the tantalising sensations being eaten alive aroused in her, but it was useless. The heat from her beaten bottom merged with the hot thrill of this forbidden delight and she felt her pussy moistening helplessly. She moaned, and her legs parted without her permission, enabling him to thrust his tongue even deeper inside her.

He raised his head and smiled at her, and she saw that the bottom half of his face was glistening shamefully with her juices.

Kneeling more comfortably between her open thighs, Habib thrust two fingers up inside her, and she moaned again. When he pulled them out they glistened with her moisture. He anointed his erection with her slippery fluids, and then pushed his cockhead against the hot opening to her flesh. There was a moment of resistance before he slid inside her with tantalising slowness. She whimpered as she felt the full length of his erection filling her, and then cried out as he began to move urgently against her, grunting like a boar in heat as he pulled his shaft out, only to ram it home again so hard that her breasts quivered beneath his thrusts.

Moaning, she arched her back and took him deep inside her, wantonly surrendering herself to the experience. His fat buttocks clenching and unclenching he rode her faster and harder, his bloated belly rolling with the effort. Then he gave one last tremendous thrust, and she felt him swell and shudder as he came. She cried out as his ejaculation pushed her senses over some mysterious edge, and tossed her head from side to side on the silk pillows as she climaxed with a blinding force that for a wonderful moment swept all her conscious thoughts away.

When Branna awoke, she discovered the crushing pressure on her chest was Habib snoring on top of her. Nausea and disgust swept over her as she tried to wriggle out from beneath his sweaty bulk, and her struggles woke him too.

Lifting himself off her, he undid her bindings and shoved her to the floor. 'Get dressed, bitch, time to go back to your kennel,' he grunted.

Avoiding his eyes, she pulled the dirty tunic over her nakedness, and did not look up when the door opened and the old man came to take her back to the hold.

She followed him with her head bent in shame, and allowed him to chain her again without protest. She had behaved like an animal. She deserved no better.

Branna awoke again with a start and sat up, staring around in confusion. For a moment she did not know where she was, and then it all came flooding back to her. She groaned in despair remembering Habib's sweaty body crushing hers, and buried her face in her hands in a vain attempt to hide her disgrace.

Then the world tilted violently, jolting her out of her self-pity. The floor shuddered and heaved beneath her, and she was forced to grab onto her chains to stop herself from sliding into the filthy straw.

'What is it?' Tallis muttered, opening her eyes. She dragged herself upright, and looked around with bleary eyes. 'What's going on?' All around them the straw rustled as the rest of the prisoners awoke to the knowledge that something was amiss, and whispers and wails of fear filled the hold.

'I don't know,' Branna muttered. There was a long grinding rattle, and for a terrifying moment she thought the ship was sinking, until she realised it was only the sound of the anchor being raised. 'I... I think we're sailing,' she said. Above her she could hear a senseless cacophony of noises, and she strained her ears until she was able to make out the distinct sounds of men shouting orders, the slap of bare feet on the deck, the creak and groan of ropes straining, and then finally a huge crack like giant hands clapping that could only be the sails unfurling. 'Yes, we are,' she gasped, 'we're moving!' A strange mix of emotions churned inside her; relief to be leaving behind everything that had happened since Cerdoc's death, and fear of what horrors were to come.

The deck shuddered and groaned again as the ship turned slowly, and began making its way out of the harbour into the open sea. At first the regular rise and fall was soothing, but as the waves grew rougher the first tendrils of nausea made their presence felt inside Branna. Her stomach began to feel queasy and she tried desperately to concentrate her thoughts on something else, but to no avail. Then she caught sight of the pannier left by the men the night before, the water in it slopping back and forth with the movement of the ship, and the colour drained from her face as she bent over and threw up.

And she was not the only one; the heavy air was thick with the sound of retching and the smell of vomit, and when evening came, marked by the arrival of food and drink, she managed to force down a mouthful of water, but immediately spewed it back up, fell back groaning, and closed her eyes.

'Aren't you going to eat anything?' Tallis asked her, enthusiastically stuffing food into her mouth. 'There's meat tonight.'

Branna opened one eye and glared at her with as much passion as she could muster. 'If I survive, I'm going to kill you,' she whispered.

Tallis laughed. 'Cheer up, it won't last forever.'

Ignoring her, Branna rolled over onto her side and fell into a fitful sleep.

Tallis was right, however. By the third day Branna awoke light-headed and ravenously hungry. The nausea was, blessedly, gone.

'Here.' Tallis rummaged inside her tunic. 'I saved this for you.' She produced a hunk of bread.

Branna gnawed on it, but could not swallow it. Her mouth was so dry her tongue felt like a strip of old leather. She had to have water. Thankfully, the pannier still lay where it had been discarded. Crawling as far as her chains would permit, she stretched to reach it. Her clawing fingers finally caught the edge and she pulled it towards her, careful not to spill any of the dregs. Flecks of straw floated on the surface and the water looked foul, but she drank it anyway.

'That's the worst of the journey over,' Tallis predicted. 'I listened when they brought the food last night. They think we'll be in port in two days' time.'

But Tallis was wrong. That night a storm blew up and they were forced to ride it out. Nothing in Branna's experience had prepared her for this. The ship rose to the top of the massive waves, and then plunged beneath them again. Screams of panic and pain filled the hold as the chained prisoners were tossed about like straws in the wind. She and Tallis clung to each other, hanging on to their chains for dear life as the boards of the ship shrieked and groaned and water seeped between the joints. Branna was sure they were all going to drown like rats in a trap.

When dawn came, and the storm finally passed, there was a new stench in the air - the smell of death. Two prisoners had died in the night, too weak to stand up to this final test of endurance. Then the hold hatch opened, and Habib himself descended to inspect the damage.

'What a waste of good profit,' he grumbled, nudging a corpse with his toe. 'Have them thrown overboard before they start to stink too much.'

His men rushed to obey him. The bodies were carted away unceremoniously, and Branna thought she heard faint splashes as they were disposed of.

She glared at Habib, her fists clenched in impotent fury. *Callous* bastard! One day he would pay for this, by all the gods, he would pay. The next time he ordered her be brought to his cabin, she vowed, she would kill him with her bare hands.

But the opportunity never arose. There were no more storms, and Habib had either lost interest in her or was too busy to indulge his lusts. Several days passed uneventfully before they at last arrived at their destination.

The first Branna knew of it was when a rough hand shook her awake. 'Move your arse, you lazy bitch. On your feet!' The order was followed by a swift kick.

Rubbing her thigh where the blow had landed, she hauled herself up, and immediately noticed the ship had stopped its constant pitching and tossing and was bobbing gently at anchor. The door of the hold was open, and bright fresh sunshine was pouring into the fetid space.

When the other prisoners were all on their feet, the crewman returned to Branna and Tallis, lifted their chains from the bulkhead, and attached them to each other. His companions did the same with the other slaves, until they were all linked together. Then, staggering and stumbling, the prisoners began to move towards the ladder. There was the sound of a whip cutting through the air, followed by a scream of pain, as one man did not walk fast enough to please their captors.

Up on deck, savouring the sweetness of the fresh air, Branna looked around her in fascination, apprehension temporarily replaced by curiosity. On the quayside richly dressed merchants bickered and bargained, slaves and seamen loaded and unloaded casks and bales and barrels, the breeze was heavy with the scent of salt and tar, fish and spices, and there was the almost musical ringing of voices speaking over half-a-dozen different languages. The people wore light, bright clothing and their exposed limbs were brown rather than white like her own. The sun beating down on her shoulders was stronger than the sun of her homeland, and the air was warmer and drier. A fierce wave of homesickness washed over her and she yearned for the cool grey light of her native land. She turned to Tallis for comfort, and shrieked as a bucket of cold water hit her full in the face.

'Gotcha!' one of the sailors said gleefully.

Gasping with shock, Branna wiped her eyes and stared through the water dripping down her face. The man had scooped up another bucketful and was aiming for her again. The thin wool of her tunic was sodden, clinging to her like a second skin and revealing the hard buds of her nipples.

The seaman eyed her appreciatively. 'Cleans up nice, don't she?' He swung the bucket again, water arced through the air, and she and Tallis cried out as a second deluge followed the first, thoroughly soaking them both. Around them, all the other prisoners were also being washed down.

At last the ordeal was over. Branna shivered, shook back her wet hair, and waited for whatever was to come next.

Habib himself appeared on deck and looked his stock over with a calculating eye. 'Excellent,' he mused. 'Now take them to the holding pens and see that they are properly fed and watered.'

Branna fumed inwardly. He might as well have been speaking about a load of cattle.

Barking orders, and using the whip to make sure they were obeyed, a number of sailors organised the slaves into a shambolic, shuffling, dispirited column. Hampered by their chains, they scuffled awkwardly down the gangplank and onto the quay, where they were herded towards a long low building at the edge of the harbour area. They were crowded inside, separated again, and chained to the walls. Even though she was at last back on solid land, the floor beneath Branna's feet still seemed to be moving, and she swayed giddily.

'At least it's not as bad as the hold,' commented Tallis, looking around almost appreciatively. The large space was bright and airy, and the straw on the floor was freshly laid.

Branna, however, was not so impressed. 'Do you think because a prison is clean it is no longer a prison?' she snapped with venom.

'No,' Tallis replied quietly and reasonably, 'but if I am to avenge what was done to my family I must grow strong again, and to that end I shall make the best of whatever the gods choose to send me. Today they have sent shelter and a roof over my head, and hopefully something decent to eat, as I am starving.'

Branna smiled at her. Tallis was right. They might be nothing but livestock now, but even the mildest beast can turn and rend its keeper if properly nourished. She, too, would bide her time and build her strength.

The doors swung open and two men entered the building rolling a barrel before them, followed by two more men carrying trays of bread and baskets full of fruit and cheese. They dispensed everything quickly and efficiently, and left.

The captives fell on the food with greedy hunger. The bread and cheese were fresh, they had been given watered wine instead of merely water, and the fruit tasted like heaven to palates long deprived of anything sweet. Branna and Tallis ate sparingly, not wishing to make themselves sick by indulging in too much too soon, but others threw caution to the wind and stuffed themselves until their bellies were swollen. It was a mistake, for they were soon paying for their indiscretion with groans of discomfort interspersed with the sound of retching.

By morning, two more prisoners were dead.

'Fools,' Habib snarled as their bodies were dragged away. 'More delays and more profit gone!' He glared around him at the survivors. 'Cut rations in half,' he ordered, 'I want no more losses.'

It was harsh treatment, but it worked. After three days, when Habib performed his daily inspection, his fat face creased in a smile of satisfaction.

'Excellent,' he murmured, rubbing his hands together. 'All seem in good condition.' His eyes fell on Branna and Tallis, and his smile became lecherous. He turned to the man beside him as he pointed towards the girls. 'Have those two brought to my lodgings this evening. Tonight I celebrate, and tomorrow we leave for Rome.'

CHAPTER 3

The girls exchanged dismayed glances as their obese master departed. The doors were open to allow the passage of air, and Branna sat with her back against the wall gazing longingly at the strange new world outside, wishing she were free to explore it. There were fewer people about now, the heat of the day having sent most of them to their homes, or to cool and shadowy taverns, but it was still busier than any place she had ever seen before. In her *oppida*, everyone knew everyone else, and a stranger was an exciting event. Here *everyone* was a stranger to her, and she watched the ever-changing scene with fascination.

An old woman, her face as brown and wrinkled as a walnut, went past leading a donkey. Its panniers were laden, and when the poor creature balked the crone beat it with a stick, snarling something incomprehensible.

Two merchants paused in the shadow of the doorway, waving their hands about in extravagant gestures and exchanging heated words. The argument continued until the older man shrugged, sighed in resignation, and handed over a fat leather purse. The younger man nodded and accepted it, and suddenly they were both all smiles. As they turned away, the one holding the purse caught Branna's eye, grinned at her, and winked.

She blushed, looking away, and then a flicker of bright colour caught her eye. She looked up again, and saw a girl of about her own age dressed as gaudily as a butterfly strolling back and forth in front of the door. Her hips moved provocatively beneath her flimsy skirt, and she smiled and murmured something to every man who passed her, pouting when they shook their heads.

Eventually she was successful and a smiling sailor responded to her proffered charms. There was some brisk haggling, several coins changed hands, and then the girl pulled him into the shelter of the doorway. From her position Branna could see it all, and she gaped as the young whore hoisted her skirts above her hips and spread her legs for her client. He groped at her breasts, fumbled at his groin, then gripped her buttocks and entered her, his hips jerking as he took her roughly against the wall like a dog humping a bitch. Only seconds later his whole body stiffened, and it was all over. Looking around, he adjusted his clothing and walked away without a backward glance.

Unconcerned, the girl calmly settled her skirts around her again, smoothing them against her hips. Then she caught Branna's horrified stare and flung her head back haughtily. 'What do you think you're looking at, you stupid cow?' she demanded. She ran her eyes over Branna, lingering on the chains at her wrists and ankles, and her hard mouth twisted in a disdainful smile. 'Think you're better than me, do you? Well, you're wrong. At least I'm not a slave. I can choose who fucks *me*.' She spat in the dust and sauntered off, her nose in the air, in search of her next customer.

Branna stared after her. The girl's words had pierced her to the heart like a poisoned arrow. She was right. She might be a common dockside whore with nothing to her name but the clothes on her back, but she had something Branna did not - she had *freedom*. And it suddenly dawned on her that, as a slave, she no longer possessed the one thing even the poorest beggar starving in the gutter owned - her own body.

She sagged against the wall, feeling sick at heart. She closed her eyes and tried to shut out the heat and the dust and the noise of the quay. Half dozing, she let her mind roam free. She was not in a strange country, penned up like an animal awaiting slaughter, she was running on her own hillside, her bare feet damp with the early morning dew, and Cerdoc was running beside her... her lips curved in a wistful smile, and she could almost feel the cool wind in her hair...

A sharp kick in the side brought her spitefully back to reality. She opened her eyes and found herself staring up into the face of the old man from the ship. 'On your feet, girl.' He nudged Tallis forcibly with his foot as well. 'And *you*, up.'

Startled, Branna realised the sun was setting. The sky had faded from bright blue to indigo, and a few early stars were already beginning to twinkle.

Tallis yawned and scratched, blinking like a sleepy owl as Branna stumbled to her feet, and stood by meekly as the old man unlocked their shackles from the wall. Then, prodding them with the handle of his small whip, he herded them towards the door. They shuffled forward awkwardly, the chains between their ankles hindering their progress, much to his annoyance.

'Get a move on,' he muttered impatiently, flicking them with his whip.

Branna yelped as the thin leather seared across her bottom, stinging her even through her tunic. She tried to move faster, tripped, and nearly fell. Cringing in expectation of the next blow she straightened up, and discovered that if she took quick but small steps she could manage better.

Outside, the dock was quiet. The ships rode at anchor, swathed in darkness apart from the solitary lamp burning on their bows and bobbing gently with the movement of the sea. As they left the harbour behind them more light spilled out from the houses and taverns crowding the narrow alleyways, and through open doors and windows Branna caught brief glimpses of other people's lives - men drinking and dicing at rough wooden tables, and a woman sweating over her hearth as she prepared the evening meal with children squabbling at her feet - snippets of ordinary lives she thoroughly envied.

Eventually the old man halted in front of a building slightly larger than its neighbours. It was whitewashed, and set back from the rest of the street in a small courtyard. Beside the arched gateway leading into the court hung a wooden sign with a picture of a woman painted on it. Branna stared at it. The woman was naked to the waist, but where her lower body should have begun there was a long curved fishtail. She had no time to wonder about it, however, as the old man pushed them into the courtyard.

It was a pretty place, with fig trees to provide a cool shade in the midday heat, and there was a wooden bench beside a small fountain. The tinkling of the water was soothing, and Branna longed simply to sit down beneath the stars, close her eyes and forget everything that had happened. But another prod in the ribs brought home the fact that her wishes meant nothing, and as she and Tallis stumbled forward, the door of the house swung open, spilling light into the courtyard.

'About time, too,' snapped the dumpy little woman silhouetted on the doorstep. 'The master and his guests are growing impatient. This way.' She led them inside and up a narrow staircase. On the landing she threw open another door, and the girls were pushed into a room that was empty except for a tub of water, a small wooden table and a narrow couch. The old man followed them in, unlocked their shackles, and then left without another word.

'Wash and change,' the woman instructed them curtly, wrinkling her nose as she took in their appearance. 'There are cleaning materials there.' She indicated the table. 'Use them. Once you're bathed, I'll return to take you to the master.' She bustled out, leaving them completely alone.

'Look at all this!' Tallis exclaimed, examining the contents of the table. 'Scented oils, a *strigil*, drying cloths...' She leaned over and trailed a finger through the water in the tub. 'And the water's hot, too!'

'What's *this* for?' Branna held up the *strigil* in bewilderment. The blunt blade looked like some sort of instrument of torture to her.

'To clean ourselves with, of course, it's the Roman custom. We wash ourselves in the hot water, apply the oil, and then scrape it off.'

'So how do you know all this?' Branna asked curiously.

'My brother's wife was an escaped slave from one of the villas our Roman masters built for themselves. She said they bathed all the time, and had running water and heat all year round, even when snow lay on the hills.' She lifted a sceptical eyebrow. 'Though I doubt that. Anyway, I'm going to make the best of it. I can't remember the last time I was truly clean.' She quickly shed her tunic, climbed into the tub, and slid beneath the water, moaning in ecstasy as the scented heat engulfed her.

'Don't just stand there,' she said when she resurfaced, 'scrub my back and then I'll do the same for you. Then we'll oil ourselves and take turns at scraping.'

Branna found a lump of coarse material with holes in it, and carried it into the tub with her. The fragrantly steaming water felt divine as she sank to her knees behind her new friend.

'That's a sponge,' Tallis explained. 'You scrub my back with it... ooh, that's wonderful!' She sighed with pleasure. 'Down a bit... that's right, right there...'

Branna grinned wickedly, and squeezed the sponge over Tallis's head.

The other girl giggled and splashed her. 'Your turn now,' she said, stepping out of the bath.

Branna settled comfortably back against one side of the tub and then slid beneath the water, feeling her hair floating around her like seaweed. When she surfaced she received a sopping sponge right in the face.

'That'll teach you,' Tallis giggled happily. 'Come on, lean forward and I'll do *you* now.' She applied the sponge vigorously to Branna's back. 'There,' she announced. 'Now you soak for a bit while I oil myself.'

Branna relaxed, and watched through half-closed eyelids as Tallis poured a little of the perfumed oil into her palm and then began rubbing it all over her body. Her skin gleamed softly in the lamplight, accentuating her slender legs and delicate breasts. In fact, if it had not been for the triangle of silky hair hiding the secret cleft of her sex, she could have passed for a pretty boy.

She caught Branna's eyes on her. 'Come on, lazy-bones,' she teased, 'get out of there. It's time to go to work.'

Obediently, Branna stepped out of the tub and shook the excess water from her skin as she wrung out her hair. 'What am I supposed to do with it?' she asked, holding up the *strigil* again and gazing at it doubtfully.

'Just run it over my skin,' Tallis explained. 'Pretend it's a razor and you're shaving me.' She spread herself facedown on the couch and closed her eyes.

Branna began to apply the strange instrument, gingerly at first, and then in long smooth strokes as she became more confident, wiping off the first layer of oil before beginning again. She marvelled at the resilience of the other girl's skin, and as she admired the smooth curves of Tallis's back and buttocks, an oddly pleasant sensation began smouldering in her belly.

'Front now,' Tallis ordered, turning over.

Branna carefully slid the *strigil* over the soft firmness of her friend's breasts, and by the time she had finished with her belly and thighs, she was feeling strangely flushed and breathless.

'Right, your turn now.' Tallis swung her legs off the couch, revealing a brief flash of rosy flesh as the lips of her sex parted. She picked up the vial of oil, poured a generous measure into her hand, and began smearing it over Branna, who gasped with pleasure beneath her firm caresses. 'Come on, don't make me do all the work,' Tallis chided her softly, and Branna followed her example by quickly working the scented oil into her own skin. 'Now lie down.'

If the feel of Tallis's hands on her had been a pleasant shock, it was nothing compared to the feel of the strigil as it glided over her body. It was like being gently stroked and licked by a large firm tongue. She closed her eyes and gave herself up to the relaxing yet stimulating experience, hoping Tallis would not notice her intensely languid reaction.

'Feels wonderful, doesn't it?'

Before Branna could answer, there was the sound of a key turning in the lock. The door opened and the short woman bustled back into the room carrying a bundle of white linen. The two girls promptly snatched up the drying cloths to cover their nakedness, and stood staring at her.

'Put these on,' the woman spat the words as she flung the bundle at them. 'And shift your lazy backsides.'

At first sight they looked like ordinary linen tunics. It was only when Branna and Tallis struggled into them that the truth revealed itself. The shifts were so short they barely covered their buttocks, and they were actually cut to reveal one entire breast. 'I cannot possibly wear this,' Branna protested.

'You'll do as you're told, and follow me,' the woman said impatiently. 'Or do I have to call my son?'

'Do what you like,' Branna retorted, tossing her head back proudly.

The woman smiled maliciously, then poked her head out into the corridor and barked an order. There was the sound of heavy footsteps, and suddenly a giant man stood on

34

the threshold. He had to stoop to enter the room, and his entire body was a mass of twisted muscles. But it was his face that was truly shocking. His dark brow protruded over empty black eyes and a slack jaw, from which hung a strand of drool.

'Bring them,' his mother commanded, and before Branna could protest she was swept over the brute's shoulder, while Tallis was lifted under one brawny arm as easily as a shepherd lifts a wayward lamb. He carried them, writhing and kicking, along the hall into another room, where he dumped them on their feet and closed the door behind him.

The two girls huddled together as they looked around them. They were standing before a low table strewn with the greasy remains of a meal, and behind them was a gilded couch. On the other side of the table sat three people - Habib, a hawk-faced man, and a strange creature who seemed neither man nor woman. The hermaphrodite was as tall as a man yet plump and devoid of body hair like a woman, its giggle girlishly high-pitched, and everything about the creature made Branna's skin crawl.

'Ah, the entertainment has arrived,' Habib declared, rubbing his plump hands together in anticipation.

'W-what do you mean?' Branna stammered.

'I mean you are here to perform for us,' Habib stated condescendingly. 'You will make love to each other while we watch.'

The girls gaped at him.

His face hardening, Habib reached behind him and produced a small whip. 'Perhaps you need to be persuaded?' he growled.

Branna squealed in pain as the lash curled around her hips, biting into the soft flesh just beneath her tunic. 'Do what you like to me!' she cried defiantly. 'You cannot make me debase myself again.' This time, she was determined he would beat her to death before she gave in to his perverted desires.

'Oh, I think I can,' her master said in a purring voice. 'I'm sure you'll change your mind when you see what happens to your pretty little friend.' He smiled, and handed the whip to the hawk-faced man. 'Omar, would you care to perform the chastisement?'

Smiling, Omar rose and walked around the table. Branna stepped protectively in front of Tallis, but he flung her aside with such force that she lost her balance and sprawled to her hands and knees. She quickly leapt to her feet again, but the disturbingly sexless creature grabbed her arms and held onto her with amazing strength while giggling insanely. She could do nothing but watch in sick fascination as Omar seized Tallis, and flung her facedown on the couch. Her tunic flipped up, and the whip descended across her tight buttocks. She shrieked and squirmed as he raised his arm and brought the whip down again. Tallis's cry was louder this time as another weal crisscrossed the first, followed immediately by a third burning trail across her delicate, freshly washed skin. As lash followed lash, her bottom turned scarlet and her outraged screams weakened to miserable whimpers.

Branna could take no more. Seeing her friend's pain was worse than enduring it herself. 'Stop!' she begged. 'We'll do whatever you say, but just stop!'

Habib waved a hand, and Omar, with evident reluctance, backed away from Tallis.

Taking a deep breath, Branna seated herself next to her friend on the couch and gently stroked her back, wincing as she felt the heat radiating from her tormented skin. Tallis moaned beneath her tender caresses, and Branna gently helped her roll over onto her back, tentatively laying her hands over the girl's small breasts as Tallis reached for hers.

They fondled each other for a few moments, and then Branna bent over and put her mouth gingerly over one of Tallis's firm nipples, running her tongue over it as though tasting an unknown berry. Tallis caught her breath, and her fingers drifted down over her friend's breasts to the tender curve of her belly and the softly furred mound of her sex below. Then, a little more boldly, mirroring each other's actions they gently parted the soft lips of their sex and slid a finger inside each other's moist and silky purse, so rich with sensations. They forgot their audience as their lips met and parted so their tongues could play together as their breaths quickened, and Branna was scarcely conscious of licking the full length of Tallis's straining body all the way down to the tantalisingly secret space between her thighs. Her tongue eagerly parted the soft petals of the other girl's labia, and lapped curiously at the firm bud of her clitoris. She was so intent on her explorations that she gasped in surprise as eager hands suddenly gripped her hips from behind and lifted them purposefully. She felt a rigid male organ prodding at her own vulva, demanding entry even as she watched Habib grab Tallis by the hair and thrust his turgid cock between her lips, his thick shaft disappearing so far into her mouth she was sure her friend would gag on it.

Branna whimpered as Omar shoved his cock inside her. Grunting with satisfaction, he rammed himself in and out of her tight slot as her breasts swayed and jiggled beneath his violent thrusts, and despite herself she could feel her own shameful pleasure mounting. The degrading sight of Tallis sucking their master's cock not only failed to put out the fire burning inside her, it actually seemed to stoke it. So with a groan of defeat she surrendered to the increasingly powerful waves of ecstasy that broke through her every time Omar's rigid manhood dove between her sex lips, her hips pushing back against him hungrily. Then she felt him shudder, impaling her as he exploded deep inside her, and the muscles of her pussy clenched around his shaft, wringing every last drop of pleasure from it as she came with him.

Silent with shame, Branna and Tallis were led back through the dark alleys to the building on the quay, where they were once again chained to the wall. They avoided each other's eyes, and when they lay down in the straw to sleep, it was as far away from each other as possible.

Branna's face flamed in the darkness recalling how she had writhed with pleasure as Tallis's lips fastened on her nipples, and how she had plunged her own tongue deep inside the hot wetness of the other girl's sex. Even now the thought made her belly tighten with desire. It would be so easy to roll over in the straw, slip her arm around Tallis's waist, and run her hand down over her smooth flesh...

With a groan of frustration Branna buried her head in her arms and tried to forget the soft, warm body lying so temptingly close to hers. Eventually she fell into an exhausted sleep, haunted by nightmares in which she was pursued by demons through twisting alleyways overgrown with thorn-covered vines clutching at her tunic as she ran...

A clattering bustle woke her, and when she raised her head she saw that Tallis and the other chained slaves were already eating breakfast. Tallis gave her a tentative smile, Branna smiled back at her, and an unspoken agreement never to mention what had happened between them was made.

'Better get something inside you,' Tallis advised, stuffing her own mouth with food.

36

'We're moving on today. Look outside.'

The quay was packed with carts, their horses chomping on their bits and shaking their heads restlessly. Some wagons were clearly filled with provisions for the journey while others were laden with bundles so carefully wrapped and padded they obviously contained something fragile and costly. It was clear Habib dealt in more than just slaves, but it was his human cargo he was interested in now. The girls cringed as his fat figure appeared on the threshold. Fortunately, however, his mind was evidently on profit today rather than pleasure. He looked around, scowled, and began barking orders. His men hurried to obey him, and began unchaining the prisoners. They dragged the weaker ones to their feet, and linked them all together again two-by-two.

Hurriedly shoving the last of the bread into their mouths, Branna and Tallis quickly stood up to avoid being kicked, and meekly allowed themselves to be re-chained to the others. Finally, everyone was linked together into one long straggling line. Habib nodded, barked one last command, and his living merchandise were marched out onto the quay to join the tail end of the caravan.

There was a flurry of last minute orders, the carters whistled and slapped the horses, wheels rumbled over the cobbles, and they began to move out. Habib, mounted on a richly caparisoned white mule, rode slowly up and down the length of the small cavalcade making sure everything had been arranged to his satisfaction.

As they stood waiting to depart Branna felt a tug of excitement at her heart, and her natural optimism began to reassert itself for the first time since her lover's death. The air was fresh, the sun was warm on her shoulders, she was young and intelligent, and a whole new world lay before her. Somewhere, somehow, she would find an opportunity to escape. And even if she did not, surely there were other ways to win her freedom. She was accustomed to hard work, and even in her remote *oppida* she had heard stories of slaves who earned their freedom.

Then the cart directly in front of her began to move, pulling the chain taut and jerking the line of slaves along behind it. Thankfully the ankle chains had been removed so it was easy to walk, and by the time they reached the main street the procession of slaves had fallen into a ragged but steady rhythm.

Apart from grubby children and the occasional dog running alongside the straggly column, few people bothered to look at them as they passed. It was a busy port and caravans of slaves setting off on the long overland route to Rome were a common sight. The occasional group of young men would eye the younger female slaves lustfully, but even their interest was fleeting.

Branna, on the other hand, was fascinated by everything she saw - the bustling street markets packed with thrifty housewives looking for a bargain; the tiny booths selling everything from jewellery to leather belts and homespun cloth; and the small crowded hovels near the quay giving way to larger houses set in their own tree-filled courtyards. Her spirits soared as they set out on the open road, and keen to keep his wares in the best possible condition to ensure maximum profit, Habib made sure they did the journey in easy stages. Nevertheless, the first few days were hard. The slaves were unaccustomed to constant marching. Their bare feet blistered, their skin reddened beneath the unrelenting sun, and a few more of them fell prey to the flux and were hastily tossed into a shallow grave by the side of the road. But after the fourth day there were no more casualties, and the prisoners fell into a mindless rhythm that seemed to go on forever.

They walked until the sun was at its highest, then ate and rested for a while afterwards in whatever shade was available. When it became cooler, they travelled until the first stars appeared in the sky, and then made camp for the night. Habib's tent would be erected first, then fires were lit and the great cauldrons set up. Food was plentiful, with grain and lentils from the provision carts supplemented by fresh fruit and vegetables bought cheaply from the small farms they passed. Habib's men alleviated the boredom of the march by hunting whenever they could, so most nights there were rabbits to be added to the pot and, if they were lucky, a small deer.

Usually they camped beside a stream or river, and the slaves would be taken in small groups to bathe while Habib's men lounged on the bank and watched over them as they washed. At first, Branna had been reluctant to strip in front of them and tried to hide herself, shamed by their lewd comments, but the sheer pleasure of cool water washing the dust from her hot skin after a long day's trek soon outweighed her modesty. After the first few times she flung her clothes off without a second thought, scrubbed her tunic, hung it to dry from a branch, and then threw herself into the river, where she would float happily on her back, her hair trailing around her like a sunlit halo, her breasts floating above the surface like pale islands.

Afterwards the prisoners sat around their fires talking, and gradually Branna and Tallis got to know some of their fellow captives. They were a motley crew, each with his or her own tale to tell of how they arrived at this sorry pass. Some were Trinovantes and Iceni like themselves and had been captured in the aftermath of Boudicca's rebellion. Others had always been slaves and were merely exchanging one master for another. Two unfortunate sisters had been sold to pay off their family's debts.

Finally, Habib's men would order them to sleep and they would curl up around the fires and fall into an uneasy slumber. For the first few nights Branna forced herself to stay awake, hoping the guards might drift off during their watch, but whenever she stole a glance at them they were still leaning on their spears and talking in low voices as they surveyed the camp. There was little hope of escape, so she resigned herself to the situation and let herself enjoy some badly needed rest. Only one terror haunted her, that some night she and Tallis would be shaken awake and ordered to Habib's tent to satisfy his foul lusts. Yet it seemed he, too, was exhausted at the end of each day's march, and so even this fear gradually faded.

Day after day merged into a kind of dreamy limbo while Branna's skin turned from white to pale gold and her hair lightened even more in the sun. Only the changing scenery marked the passing of time as they marched up through Gaul and into Italia. The air became hotter and drier. Farmland became hillier and stonier, woodlands sparser. The language they overheard as they travelled through small towns became softer and more liquid. Then the towns grew increasingly larger, and one day Branna woke and sensed a strange new tension in the air. The morning meal was hurried, the guards seemed to have shaken off the apathy that had overtaken them during the long journey, and Habib's harried expression was replaced by one of smug satisfaction as he rode up and down the ranks, urging them onwards with what almost seemed like excitement.

They reached the summit of a hill, and Branna gasped in wonder at the view. A massive city sprawled across the plain and over seven hills like a pampered courtesan spread-eagled on her couch eager to take on all comers. There were tiers upon towering tiers of houses and gardens and plazas and market places and roads, and acres of marble gleamed white as bleached bones beneath the hot sun. The infamous city hung before her dazzled eyes, a mirage of power and wealth and the hub of the civilised world - Rome.

Branna had expected their cavalcade to arrive at the gates of Rome by mid-morning, but the distance was deceptive. All day they marched across the plain beneath the penetrating sun, and despite Habib's chivvying, by evening they had only reached the foothills below the city.

They made camp for the last time in a grove by the bank of the Tiber. Branna and her fellow slaves sat silently around the small fires. Tomorrow they would enter Rome and the slave market, and chances were they would never see each other again. The night was strangely still and sounds carried far - the usual eerie music of nocturnal insects, hooting owls, and furtively moving and squeaking rodents in the undergrowth. But then she also became aware of a constant low humming reminiscent of a working beehive. Puzzled, she wondered what it was until it finally dawned on her that what she was hearing was the distant sound of Rome. The thought was strangely terrifying. Did these cruel people never sleep? Staring up at the city's looming silhouette, she became aware of a dim and pulsing glow, and realised it was the light of thousands of torches burning against the darkness. She shivered. Surely it was tempting the gods to turn night into day like this.

'Why are you trembling?' Tallis whispered. 'Are you cold? Do you want to share my blanket?'

The offer of human warmth was irresistible. 'Thank you, yes.'

Tallis lifted the corner of her blanket invitingly. It was already warm from her body, and Branna slid gratefully beneath it. She slipped her arm beneath her friend's neck, and Tallis nestled her head in the crook of her shoulder. They lay snuggled together, looking silently up at the alien stars, and the chill gradually left Branna and she drifted off to sleep.

Dawn was barely beginning to lighten the sky when they were awoken and ordered to their feet. Around them the other slaves were stretching and yawning. Food and water were thrust at them with instructions to make haste. They ate quickly, saw to their bodily needs, and were on the road again when the sun was still resting on the horizon.

Blinking sleepily, Branna realised they were only part of a great river of people making their way into the city. She saw farmers escorting mule-drawn carts heavily laden with produce; other traders like Habib leading their own strings of weary slaves; richly dressed merchants; ordinary people on foot on their way to the markets; and rich noblemen and women reclining on litters born by slaves. She gasped in astonishment at the sight of three great humped animals, the likes of which she had never seen, or even dreamed of, before, their tall sides laden with baskets and bundles as they moved with stately slowness, their great flat feet raising clouds of dust with every step. It seemed as if the whole world was making its way to Rome.

The road, which had gradually widened the closer they got to the city, grew even broader. Hawkers lined the way, accosting the travellers with offers of cheap goods, and there were women, too, peddling their flesh with painted smiles and coy gestures of invitation. Then the sound of a horn rent the air, and to Branna's astonishment Habib's men began to hurry them to the side of the road. Everyone else was following suit, hastily clearing the way. The horn wailed a second time, and when the annoying sound died away, she heard what sounded like the muted roar of thunder. Straining her eyes she made out a cloud of dust on the horizon, and gradually line after line after line of marching men became visible within it. As they approached their tramping feet drowned out every other sound. Horsehair plumes bobbed in the wind, polished armour glittered in the sun and red cloaks swung from stiff shoulders as grim-faced men marched towards the city in a seemingly endless line looking neither to right or left.

It seemed a very long time before the dust settled and the sound of marching feet faded away, and it was another weary hour before they came to a halt again just below the looming walls of Rome and the massive gates leading into the infamous city. Branna could make out the figures of soldiers guarding the gates as they checked papers and the contents of carts before waving people into the city. Very slowly the line of travellers shuffled forward, a few frustrating steps at a time. Branna was perspiring, dust clung to her skin, and she felt they would never reach their goal.

Finally there was just one more cart, one more group of merchants, one more litter ahead of them, and then it was their turn.

Smiling enthusiastically, Habib exchanged a few words with the guard, who ran a jaded eye over the string of slaves before waving them through the gate.

If Branna thought Rome was magnificent from outside the walls, the reality of the city enclosed within them eclipsed all her imaginings. It was huge beyond belief; the crowds of travellers that seemed so large on the road dispersing like drops of water in the ocean. There was so much to look at she could not take it all in at once, and her neck hurt from craning it as she tried to see everything.

Enormous streets were packed with litters, donkeys, carts and servants rushing about their masters' business. There were countless bustling marketplaces, and temples large and small adorned with statues and fountains all made of gilded marble. The whole scene blurred into one great glittering kaleidoscope of heat and colour, sound and smells, assaulting all her senses at once.

She was so dazed by it all that she scarcely noticed how far they had walked until a great spread of low stone buildings and pens loomed before them. At first she thought it was an animal market, then she realised it was not beasts she saw milling about but people of all ages and races. The only thing they had in common were the chains dangling between their wrists and ankles, and she knew they had finally reached their destination - the great slave market of Rome.

There was a brief interlude while Habib dickered at the entrance to the market, and then once all was satisfactorily settled, his living property was led into one of the long buildings, which was much like the one at the quayside where they had originally docked, all except for the massive scale. Despite its size, it was already three-quarters full of slaves of all shapes and sizes and colours. Branna stopped short, and stared in amazement at a group of young men and women, their skin dark and gleaming. She had never seen *black* people before, and the sight arrested her.

A shove in the small of the back urged her on, and the now familiar routine of unchaining wrists and ankles, and re-chaining them to walls, was accomplished with the rapidity of long practice. Habib disappeared, and Branna made herself comfortable as she prepared for another long day of boring inactivity while she awaited her fate.

They barely had time to relax, however, before Habib bustled back into the building with two other men in tow. One of his companions was tall and thin, with dark-brown skin and a hooked nose, while the other was short and plump and scurried behind him like a fussy hen, clutching pen and ink and a sheaf of parchment. She stood up again so she could see better, and watched as the tall man ordered a slave to his feet and began examining him, checking his ears, his eyes and his mouth before running his hands quickly over the rest of his body as the small man scribbled furiously on his parchment. Once the inspection was over there was a brief discussion, during which Habib waved his arms about passionately as the scribe kept writing. Then the little man removed the sheet of parchment, attached it to a short length of twine, and hung it around the slave's neck.

'Certificate of fitness,' a voice whispered in her native tongue. 'Got to make sure yer in good working order 'fore they buys yer.'

She turned her head, and found herself looking into an ancient and weather-beaten face. The owner of the voice leaned on the broom he was pushing, and grinned toothlessly at her. 'No returns, yer see, not unless yer got the falling sickness.'

'Who are you?' she demanded. 'And how do you know my language?'

'My name's Gran, and I been here a long time, but not so long I can't remember my own tongue, or tell a good Iceni girl when I see one.'

One of the overseers bellowed at him to get on with his work, and his grin vanished as he began sweeping again with renewed vigour. 'You just keep yer head down, girl, and do whatever they tells yer,' he advised quietly as he moved away. His tunic had slipped from one of his bony shoulders, and a cold finger touched Branna's spine as she saw the livid scars of old whip marks on his wrinkled skin. But she did not have time to brood on them as the physician had reached her, and she was forced to submit to his examination as the scribe scribbled his observations. Then the square of parchment was hung around her neck, and they moved on. She lifted the stiff paper and stared down at the strange black marks, wondering what they meant.

This brief excitement over, the rest of the day dragged on. Exhausted by inaction and fruitless speculation, Branna fell asleep right after the evening meal.

In the morning food was handed out with orders to eat quickly, and afterwards, much to her amazement, their feet were dusted with chalk. It was only later she discovered this was to indicate they were new slaves. Men shouted orders and groups of prisoners were hustled past her and out into the open yard, where a crowd had gathered around a raised dais. And as she watched in horror, the first slaves were stripped naked and pushed up onto the stand.

The visions of that horrible morning were burnt into her brain forever. Children shrieked as they were torn from their weeping mothers, and a fat old woman sobbed with shame as the crowd laughed at and mocked her. Young men cringed as ancient lechers groped their toned bodies before they placed their bids, and led them away to a future of unimaginable degradation.

Tallis went before her, and Branna winced in sympathy for her friend as an evil-faced old woman examined her, sliding her hands over her breasts and prodding her between her thighs before nodding with satisfaction. The crone's expression changed to one of rage, however, as several men bid against her, raising the price, but she persevered and finally hauled her new property away. Tallis flung one last despairing glance over her shoulder at Branna, and then disappeared into the crowd.

When her turn came, Branna closed her eyes and bit her lip as her tunic was wrenched from her body and she was thrust naked onto the dais. Suppressing her fear, she opened her eyes again, straightened her shoulders, and gazed defiantly back at the crowd.

Greedy eyes stared back at her, and a murmur of appreciation ran through the buyers at the sight of her lithe young body with its proud breasts, narrow waist and curvaceous hips. A group of young men, who seemed to be there more for entertainment than anything, hooted and catcalled their appreciation, making her blush with shame.

But if that was bad, much worse was to come.

Several men pushed their way onto the dais, and her skin crawled as they took turns examining her like an animal. Her mouth was forced open and her teeth inspected. Odious hands crawled up and down her legs, and she bit back a whimper of pain as vile fingers forced themselves inside her pussy. She attempted to squirm away from this cold invasion of her body, and then shrieked as a stinging cut from the auctioneer's whip made her buttocks jump and quiver.

At long last she was left alone on the dais again and the bidding began at five hundred *sesterces*. It rose swiftly, until only two men were left bidding against each other. She looked at the first man, and shivered. His face was puffy with drink and debauchery, and a lizard-like tongue darted out to lick his thin lips as he raised the bid yet again. His eyes were reptilian, flat and cold, and she could read death in their pale depths. Praying to all her gods that she would not fall into his hands, she glanced fearfully towards the other much more decent-looking man, and her legs went weak with relief as he raised his hand again. The auctioneer glanced back at the toad-like bidder, who shook his head, spat in the dust, and turned away with a final venomous glare at her, as if it was somehow her fault he had lost.

Her buyer made his way through the crowd, picked her tunic up off the ground, and flung it at her as she stepped off the dais. 'Cover yourself, girl,' he commanded.

Gratefully she hid her nakedness, and looked up into his cool face waiting for him to speak again.

'I am Fabius, major-domo to Marcus Cornelius,' he informed her.

Branna gawped at him as it sank in that this tall aristocratic man was a slave, too.

'You will come with me,' he said coldly. 'And do not even think of running away. Our master is a fair man, but he does not take kindly to disobedience.' He turned away, and Branna followed after him feeling sick at heart. The last thing she saw as she left the slave market was Habib's smirking face as he counted the *sesterces* that had cost a proud young woman her freedom. Her life of slavery had truly begun.

CHAPTER 4

Her stomach churning with apprehension, Branna trailed behind Fabius with her eyes lowered, barely noticing the busy booths they passed or the crowds jostling them. There was no point in running away. To where would she run? Where could she hide?

How would she live?

Miserably, she trudged on as they left the bustling marketplaces behind them. The streets were quieter now, with imposing houses set back in their own gardens and courtyards in which slaves wearing metal collars around their necks as badges of their servitude tended plants and trees. Her spirits rose a little seeing them. They looked well fed, and showed no obvious signs of mistreatment. Perhaps her new life would not be so hard to bear after all. But this brief flicker of hope was destined to die almost as quickly as it was born.

As she watched an elderly gardener stumbled, and the heavy earthenware jug he was carefully tipping water from crashed to the floor of the courtyard, shattering loudly. The echoes had barely died away before his master, who had been sitting reading in the shade, rose to his feet and advanced on him. Then, before Branna's horrified gaze, he subjected the unfortunate slave to a barrage of blows that left him grovelling in abject misery on the ground. The beaten old man then limped away, still stammering out apologies for his clumsiness, a trickle of blood staining his white hair.

She felt sick. *This* was the mighty civilisation of Rome? In her tribe the elderly were treated with respect, not beaten like dogs. Fabius had not even noticed the incident, or if he had, he took it so much for granted that it meant nothing to him.

At long last, just when she thought they were going to keep walking forever, he halted before a house larger than all the other ones around it. For a moment she thought perhaps it was a small temple. Even its courtyard seemed more ornate than most, with several flourishing trees and a marble bench beside a lily pond in which colourful fish swam languidly amidst the leaves. White columns flanked the portico, and a young Nubian slave lounged before them, his skin a startling black against his white tunic. At sight of them he drew himself to attention, and Fabius nodded briefly at him as he strode by with Branna scurrying behind him, the heels of her leather sandals slapping on the polished marble floor.

Inside the house she stopped and stared around. They were in a large open area with rooms running off it on all sides. In the centre of the space was a shallow pool with a couch at one end, and directly above the water there was an opening in the roof. There was no other furniture, but the walls were decorated with frescoes of strange sea monsters cavorting in impossibly blue waves, and what looked like a small shrine stood near the entrance.

Fabius saw her look of awe, and smiled at her for the first time. 'The *atrium*,' he announced, waving a proprietary arm around him with as much pride as if he owned the house himself. He pointed to the pool. 'The *impluvium*.' He then indicated the opening in the ceiling. 'The *compluvium*. It allows rain to fill the pool.'

Branna felt like a stupid child as she tried to follow his words, repeating them to herself beneath her breath in an effort to memorise them. The sooner she improved her knowledge of the language of her masters, the easier it would be for her to survive.

The brief lesson over, Fabius indicated that she should follow him again as he strode towards one of the rooms opening on the left. When they entered it he cleared his throat and bowed.

'I have brought the new slave, Mistress Lavinia,' he announced quietly.

'Very good, Fabius,' a bored voice replied.

Branna stared at her new mistress. The woman was seated before a table while one slave girl arranged her dark hair into a pile of ornate curls on her head, and a second girl held up a hand mirror so she could see herself. Two more female slaves stood by holding vials of sweet-smelling perfume. Lavinia waved them away, and turned to look at Branna. Her sharp eyes quickly took in the tangled hair, dusty limbs and stained tunic.

Branna's shoulders straightened as she stared rebelliously back at the Roman matron.

Lavinia's lip curled with disdain, and she waved a languid hand at Fabius. 'Take her away and clean her up. She can start work in the *culina*.' She then turned back to her mirror with bored indifference.

Branna stared at her with impotent fury. The woman, with her pretty, discontented face and pampered body, had made her feel totally insignificant, of less value even than one of the glass vials on her dresser. Murderous hatred bubbled up inside her and she longed to fly at her new mistress and rip the smug sneer right off her pouting lips. She wanted to tear open that smooth white throat and...

Fabius's fingers dug into her arm so hard as he pulled her out of the room that she nearly cried out.

'Do you know what happens when a slave kills a master or mistress?' he demanded once they were safely out of earshot.

Branna shook her head.

'We *all* die, that's what. Not just you, and not just me for failing to prevent it. Every single slave in this house - man, woman and child - is put to death. Do you understand me?' His mouth set grimly before he added, 'And it is no easy death, either.'

Branna stared at him in disbelief, and then despair washed over her as yet another escape route closed on her forever. She could face her own death, no matter how terrible, but she could not be responsible for the deaths of others - of innocent people.

Satisfied he had made his point, Fabius let her go. 'Follow me,' he said in a more distant voice. 'I shall take you to the slave quarters, where you will clean yourself and change into more suitable attire before taking up your position in the *culina*.' He led her through to the rear of the building and the small room that housed all the slaves. There were no fancy frescoes and mosaics here, just bare whitewashed walls, a stone floor, and narrow couches that had plainly seen better days. 'Wait here,' he said, and left her alone.

Meekly seating herself on one of the couches, Branna sighed with relief as she at last took the weight off her aching feet. But she had barely eased off her sandals when two dark-haired girls entered the room, giggling and nudging one another. Branna stared at them as they subjected her to a barrage of questions, speaking so quickly she could scarcely understand a word they said, and her blank look merely seemed to amuse them even more.

'*Chloe*,' said one of the girls, pointing to herself.

'*Miriam*,' the other girl chimed in with a similar emphatic gesture.

'Um, Branna,' she replied, placing her hand over her heart.

Giggling again, Chloe put down the jug of water she was carrying and mimed washing herself, while Miriam held out a towel, a patched but clean tunic, and a new pair of sandals. Then they stood looking at her expectantly.

Branna realised they had no intention of leaving until she had performed her ablutions, so she got to her feet reluctantly and shrugged off her stained tunic, letting it fall to her feet. Then she took the proffered washcloth, dipped it in the jug of water, and scrubbed the dirt and dust from her body while the two girls eyed her fair skin and commented quietly between themselves.

Once Branna had dried herself and put on the clean tunic Chloe produced a comb, pushed her down onto the couch, and literally attacked her hair, exclaiming over its colour. Branna winced as the girl dragged the comb roughly through all her tangles, amazed the fine bone implement did not break in the process. Then, when her long mane was finally smooth, Chloe twisted it deftly into a knot at the nape of her neck, pinned it in place, and stepped back to admire her handiwork.

'That much better,' she said, nodding with satisfaction. 'You come with us now. Is time to work.'

Reluctantly, Branna got to her feet again. After everything she had been through, all she wanted was to curl up on the couch and close her eyes and go to sleep. But instead she had to accompany the two chattering girls to the *culina*, whatever *that* was.

They did not walk through the main house but rather took a side door into another garden. Unlike the one in the front courtyard, this garden was strictly practical. A gnarled olive tree, and several other trees heavy with apples and some yellow fruit Branna did not recognise, shaded beds of herbs and vegetables. And in the centre stood a dovecot, its occupants fluttering their white wings and cooing gently. 'Oh, how pretty!' she exclaimed.

Chloe and Miriam exchanged glances, and giggled yet again. 'Is not pretty, is for eating,' Chloe explained, rubbing her belly. 'Good!' She pointed towards the back of the main building, where a wooden door stood open in the heat. A pile of wicker baskets stood beside it, with a beady-eyed chicken staring out from each one. 'But we hurry now, or Clovis have us beaten.' A bellow from within made the two girls wince, and grabbing Branna by the arms they practically thrust her through the open door.

The first thing she registered was the intense heat. It had been warm outside, but this felt like stepping into a boiling cauldron. Beads of perspiration sprang out on her forehead as she regarded the culprits - two ovens lining one entire wall. A tray of hot loaves sat on a long wooden table in front of them, and a slave was pushing a second batch of dough in to be baked while another slave prepared a tray of what looked like honey-cakes. A large open fire was also burning, with several earthenware pots sitting on a gridiron placed over it, while a joint of meat hung from a hook just above the flames.

The smells hit her next, the mouth-watering aroma of fresh-baked bread and roasting meat and the tantalising hint of cooked spices, all mixed in with the pungent scent of perspiring human flesh.

Then the noise hit her and made her want to cover her ears against the deafening clatter of kitchen implements, shouted orders, the roar of live flames, and the constant chatter of gossip as the slaves went about their business. She felt dizzy with the assault to her senses, and in the centre of all this mayhem stood a huge bald man, a testament to his own skills judging by the thick layers of fat covering his body. Drops of sweat dripped off his double chins as he yelled instructions, and cuffed ears when they were not obeyed quickly enough for his liking.

Branna was dragged forward and pushed before him. 'This is the new slave, Clovis,' Miriam announced anxiously.

The man glared at Branna, his large hands on his broad hips. 'Hah!' he bellowed, looking her over disdainfully. 'Another skinny little piece. What use are you to me, girl?' he asked slowly, so she could understand him.

'I am stronger than I look,' Branna replied defiantly, glaring right back at him. 'And I work hard and well. You'll have no complaints of me.'

Clovis threw his head back and laughed, causing rolls of fat to jiggle across his massive gut. 'Well said, girl, well said.' His eyes twinkled. 'Get something inside that scrawny belly, and we'll soon see. You can start on the querning, for I need more flour.'

The rest of the day was a nightmare. Perspiration blinded Branna, and the muscles of her shoulders screamed as she turned the heavy stone to grind the grain. She gritted her teeth and ignored the pain as the thought of Clovis's derision if she failed at her first task kept her going. By the time their owner had been fed and the dishes brought back and cleaned, her eyes were closing. She was almost too fatigued to even eat her own meal. Then Chloe's elbow dug into her ribs, and she sat up with a start as a stocky man with bulky arms and shoulders entered the kitchen.

'Where's the new one?' he asked in a deep voice.

'I - I am here,' Branna mumbled warily.

'Right, you come along with me then,' he ordered.

Her heart sank; all she wanted to do was sleep, but she obediently pushed her unfinished meal away and stumbled wearily to her feet.

It was dark outside, but her guide seemed to have eyes like a cat. She followed him down through the garden to a small building she had not noticed earlier, and opening the door, he pushed her inside. The place stank of leather and hot metal, and she looked in dismay at the small furnace glowing in the corner. He turned towards her, and she cringed in fear as he suddenly put both his large hands around her neck. But he let her go almost at once, muttering something beneath his breath as he bent to rummage for something in a corner. When he turned towards her again he was holding a narrow iron collar in his hands, and before she could back away he had clicked it around her throat and locked it in place. Instinctively she tried to wrench it off, but the cold metal was immovable.

Branna cried herself to sleep that night, the slave band heavy around her neck. Chloe had translated the words engraved on it for her: *I am a runaway. Please return me to my owner.*

She could flee to the ends of the empire, but she would never be free again.

Like an animal in a trap, Branna withdrew inside herself. Her eyes lowered, and she spoke only when spoken to, obeying her orders in sullen silence. But gradually, as she became accustomed to the hated collar, she also settled into life within the household. She was no stranger to hard work, and in many ways her new existence was easier than the one she had left behind in her homeland. Life, even if it was not the life she had chosen for herself, was at least tolerable.

Thankfully she saw little of her whey-faced mistress. As the newest slave girl, most of her work was in the *culina*. She pounded spices, ground grain into flour, and fetched and carried. On a few precious occasions she was also allowed the privilege of accompanying Clovis when he attended the market first thing in the morning to choose fresh meat, vegetables and poultry. He would saunter regally through the various stalls while she and two other girls trooped behind him with baskets to carry his purchases. She relished the sights and sounds of the busy marketplace, enjoying the fresh air and the glimpse into other people's lives.

Back at the house, Clovis would pour himself a beaker of wine and issue his orders for the day, overseeing them as everyone hurried to obey him. Branna loathed it when they had fish; she hated the feel of the cold flesh and the bloody guts, not to mention the smell. Clovis presented all his dishes like works of art, and the first time her hand slipped and she damaged some of the fish's gleaming scales, she was rewarded by a swift buffet to the head that very effectively taught her to be more careful in future.

But even more loathsome was the rancid fish sauce he was so fond of. It stank to high heaven, and he seemed to use it in everything; even pears stewed in wine were treated to a dash of it. And yet, much to her surprise, it was delicious.

There were luxuries in her life, too. The fact that there was a supply of running water, both hot and cold, was a constant source of wonder to her. Summer drifted into autumn, and now that the days were cooler, slaves stoked a furnace beneath the house that sent warm air circulating through the rooms.

And most astounding of all was the *latrina*, a room beside the kitchen where you could go attend to your bodily needs. She might detest her Roman masters, but she could not help but be impressed by their ingenuity.

Her Latin was also improving. Every day she could understand more of what was being said to her, making her feel less cut off. One of the chief pleasures of her fellow slaves was gossiping, quite maliciously, about their owners. She listened avidly, anxious to learn as much as she could. When your life depended on others, it was a good idea to know as much about them as possible.

'Done at last, thank the gods,' Branna groaned one morning as she stood up from the quern stone and stretched her aching arms. 'I thought I would never finish!'

'That's nothing,' scoffed Miriam as she collected the flour. 'Just wait till the master gets home next week. You'll have to grind twice as much once he starts entertaining.'

'Where has he been?' Branna inquired with interest. Marcus Cornelius might be her owner, but she had yet to set eyes on him.

'Running his farm down south,' Miriam explained. 'He always spends the summer there, but now the harvest is in he'll be back in Rome until the spring planting, and bringing Helga with him, no doubt.'

'Helga?' Branna asked.

'His mistress,' said Miriam with relish. 'She's from one of those outlandish tribes from Germanica.' She looked at Branna speculatively. 'She looks a bit like you, come to think of it. She has the same fair skin, although she's a bit taller than you and her hair's lighter - nearly white.' She sighed enviously. 'She wears it in a great plait down her back. I wish mine was like that.'

'Is she a freewoman?'

'Of course not!' exclaimed Miriam, looking shocked. 'He could be put to death if she was. That would be adultery. No, she's just a slave the same as us, so it doesn't count.' She lowered her voice. 'But they've got a son, and there's talk that he's thinking of adopting him and making him his heir.' She grinned wickedly. 'That would put *her* nose out of joint, and no mistake.' It was obvious she was referring to their mistress. 'All *she's* ever managed to produce is one sickly little girl, and a spoilt little brat she is, too.' She nodded portentously. 'You mark my words, Mistress Lavinia is a bitch at the best of times, but she'll be unbearable now. I wouldn't be one of her personal slaves for a thousand *sesterces*.' She would have said more, but Clovis interrupted them.

'You two, stop that gossiping,' he bellowed, 'and get on with your work!'

Miriam scurried off with the flour, and Branna sighed as she cleaned yet another disgusting fish.

One afternoon she was grinding spices when one of Lavinia's handmaidens burst into the kitchen whimpering pitifully. A scarlet handprint stood out against one of her cheeks, and she was cradling her right hand against her chest.

The kitchen slaves gathered around her, eager for gossip and glad for a break in their monotonous routine. The unfortunate girl was bombarded with a chorus of questions. 'What is it? What happened? Are you badly hurt?'

'Of course she's hurt,' Clovis snarled. 'Get out of the way.' He pushed the girl down into a chair, and then took out a flask of wine. Pouring a beaker, he added two drops of poppy juice to it from a small phial, and thrust the mixture into her hand. 'Drink this,' he commanded.

She did so eagerly, and almost at once her sobbing subsided.

'Now, tell us what happened,' Clovis demanded gently.

'It was the mistress.' She sniffed and wiped her eyes. 'I dropped a bottle of her favourite perfume, and she hit my hand with the side of her mirror.' Gingerly, she held the offended member up for everyone to see, and there was a collective gasp of horror. Three of her fingers were bent at a grotesque angle and swollen beyond recognition. 'They're broken!' she moaned.

'They need to be straightened at once,' Branna declared, 'or they will heal crookedly.'

The girl blanched; a crippled slave, particularly one who relied on the nimbleness of her fingers, would soon find herself back on the market, at a considerably lowered price, and there was no telling where she might end up then.

'I need bandages and something to support them,' Branna went on briskly, and smiled encouragingly at her patient. 'This may hurt a little, but it is necessary.'

The colour drained from her faced, the girl nodded and bit her lip to keep herself from crying out as Branna dealt with her injury.

'There, that should do it,' Branna declared once she had finished binding the wounded fingers. 'But I'm afraid you won't be able to tend to the mistress for a while.'

'I know,' the girl said miserably, looking up at Clovis almost apologetically. 'She said you were to send another slave to take my place.'

He frowned. 'As if I didn't need all of them myself!' he grumbled. 'Haven't I enough to worry about already with the master due home any day now?' He looked around the circle of anxious faces, and his gaze settled on Branna. 'You seem handy with your fingers, girl, and you've proved yourself competent. You'll have to do.'

'Try and count yourself lucky,' Chloe said in a vain attempt to console her as she helped Branna out of her coarse woollen tunic and into a finer one marking her rise in status. 'The goddess Fortuna has smiled on you. This is a step up. See, you've new clothes already.'

'Only because it would offend Lavinia's aristocratic nostrils if I attended her reeking of fish sauce,' Branna muttered.

'Nonsense.' Chloe forced a smile. 'Surely you cannot prefer to stay a kitchen slave? It is a great honour to serve the mistress.'

'A dangerous honour,' Branna added dryly, 'and one I could well live without. I have already seen how well honoured my predecessor was.'

Chloe suddenly lost her temper. 'Look, there's nothing you can do about it, so you might as well accept it with good grace,' she snapped. 'Keep your eyes down and your mouth shut, unless it's to say "yes, mistress", and you'll be fine.' She smiled slyly. 'You never know, you might even earn yourself a few *peculia*.'

Branna stared at her. 'What's a peculia?'

'A *peculium* is a gift of money,' Chloe explained patiently. 'If you got enough of them, you might even be able to buy your freedom. Mind you, I can't see her ladyship giving you any. But of course, when the master begins entertaining she might lend you to her friends when they visit, and they'd be bound to give you something even if it was just to show off their wealth.'

Branna regarded her sceptically. There seemed to be far too many 'ifs' and 'buts' in the possibility of buying herself out of slavery with all these hypothetical gifts. Even if she did receive any, she would probably be fifty-years-old before she managed to scrape up enough to cover the cost of her freedom. Still, despite her cynicism, a little seed of hope insisted on blooming and spreading inside her. A possibility suddenly existed where there had been none before.

When Branna entered her mistress's room, Lavinia was lying on a couch by the window with her hand to her forehead, moaning softly. 'Pour me a glass of wine,' she commanded, waving a limp hand towards the jug. 'All that weeping and wailing has given me a dreadful headache.'

There were already two other slaves present. One was fanning her mistress while the other was tidying her dressing table.

Branna did as she was told.

Lavinia sipped the wine, and then winced theatrically and lay back again. 'Fetch me a cold compress for my head,' she said in an exhausted voice. 'This is all that wretched girl's fault...'

Tight-lipped, Branna turned on her heels and stalked from the room. Her self-control lasted until she reached the kitchen, and then she yelled, 'Selfish cow!' as she collected a clean cloth along with a bowl of cold water to soothe Lavinia's fevered brow. 'Lying there complaining! I'd like to see the pampered bitch do a hard day's work. It would probably kill her!'

Back in Lavinia's quarters she silently dipped the cloth in the cold water, and wrung it out imagining it was her mistress's neck. Careful to keep her face expressionless, she laid it on Lavinia's forehead.

The woman closed her eyes and sighed with pleasure. 'Ah, that's much better,' she said languidly.

'Will there be anything else, mistress?' Branna asked with what she hoped was suitable humility.

The cold grey eyes snapped open, and a soft white hand caught Branna a stinging blow on the cheek. 'Of course there will be, you stupid girl,' she whined. 'Did you think your duties were finished? You will kneel beside my couch and reapply the cloth as soon as it becomes warm.' She pointed to the slave who was clearing up the mess. 'Calla, fetch the lyre. Some soothing music might ease my pain a little.'

The girl scurried out of the room, reappeared with an instrument and sat in a corner, where she began to play quietly.

'Not so loud,' Lavinia snapped. 'Do you wish to make my poor head even worse?'

Obediently, the slave played even more softly, and Lavinia sighed and closed her eyes again.

Branna's knees were aching from kneeling on the stone floor by the time a change in Lavinia's breathing indicated she had fallen asleep, and she looked at the girl on the other side of the couch. 'May I leave now?' she whispered.

Without missing a beat in her constant fanning, the other slave shook her head. 'Better not,' she whispered back. 'If she wakes and finds you gone, she'll be furious. We can't do anything without her permission.'

Sighing, Branna shifted her position a little to ease the pain in her knees. Even fish-gutting was more exciting than this. She looked around the room, taking in the brilliantly coloured frescoes on the walls, the expensive cedar chest, the dressing table with its array of cosmetics and small glass vials, and the large scrolled and gilded bed frame. Profoundly bored, she then turned her attention back to her sleeping mistress. In repose, Lavinia's carefully tended face had fallen into heavy lines of discontent. Her mouth had gone slack, and a thick layer of cosmetics failed to conceal the wrinkles running from the sides of her nose to the edges of her mouth. Grey hairs showed at her temples, and beneath her fine *stola* her voluptuous body was beginning to sag. Her large breasts were slack and her belly was full and soft. She had clearly been a handsome woman once, but now she was fighting and losing the battle against the relentless ravages of time.

As if she sensed Branna's gaze upon her, Lavinia stirred and her eyes fluttered open. She sat up slowly, yawned, and swung her legs over the edge of the couch, almost knocking Branna over. 'Fetch my comb and mirror, Flaminia,' she ordered lazily. 'My hair must be done again.' She pointed to the girl playing the lyre. 'Stop that infernal row and bring me a clean *stola*.' Lastly, her haughty gaze settled on Branna. 'And you go fetch me some bread and fruit.'

Stiffly, Branna got to her feet and hurried out of the room. Back in the *culina* she filled an earthenware bowl with the choicest peaches, grapes and figs, picked up a knife and a small loaf of bread, and hurried back before she could be accused of dallying. Yet when she offered the food to Lavinia, the woman stared down her nose at her as if she was mad.

'Peel them, girl,' her mistress snapped. 'Do I have to tell you how to do everything? And pour me another glass of wine.'

Gritting her teeth Branna did as she was told, and as soon as Lavinia had finished eating Branna was sent to fetch a finger bowl.

Her mistress cleaned her hands and face, then stretched out on the couch again and smiled. 'I think I shall have some entertainment now, a little amusement to pass the time until dinner.' She pointed at Calla. 'You, go and fetch that idle black boy who tends the door. Let us see what other talents he possesses.'

Bobbing to her mistress, Calla did as she was told, returning with the Nubian slave, who stood waiting impassively for his orders.

'Come closer, boy,' Lavinia said.

He stepped up to the couch, and Branna gasped in shock as her mistress reached beneath his tunic and casually fondled his genitals. His response was instantaneous; the light material lifted as his penis swelled beneath it.

'Take off your tunic, boy' Lavinia instructed him, a little hoarsely.

Obediently he let it drop to the floor, and his manhood jutted out from the base of his belly like a thick black club, the head tight and swollen. Lavinia's hand was shockingly white against his black skin as she moved it up and down on his thick shaft. Then, smiling, she lay back again and turned her attention to Branna. 'On your knees, girl,' she commanded, 'and open your mouth.'

Branna did not, could not, move.

'Oh dear, our little Iceni maiden is shy,' the woman mocked. 'Do as you are told, girl.'

Branna shook her head stubbornly, but instead of losing her temper, Lavinia smiled and licked her lips. 'Ah, I see you need a lesson in obedience,' she said. 'Flaminia, fetch the whip.'

The girl scurried to a cupboard in the corner, and returned with a vicious-looking instrument in her hand.

The Roman matron took it from her, and ran the lashes lovingly through her fingers. 'Are you going to do as you are told, or not?' she asked Branna.

Branna stared back at her rebelliously.

'Seize her,' Lavinia snapped, and Calla and Flaminia grabbed Branna's arms.

'Do as she tells you,' Calla whispered frantically in her ear. 'It will be over soon. She will win in the end, no matter how much you struggle.'

Branna ignored her fellow slave, and glaring at Lavinia, she spat on the floor. 'Do your worst,' she hissed. 'I will never give in to you.'

'Oh, I think you will,' Lavinia mused, smiling evilly as she stood up. 'And your defiance will only make your surrender to me all the sweeter.' She tore Branna's tunic off her with one amazingly strong gesture, revealing the girl's slender body, and trailed the lashes of the whip over her breasts, clearly relishing the way her soft flesh flinched beneath their caress. 'Hold her tight,' the mistress commanded, and stepped around behind her.

Branna struggled to free herself, and then the world exploded in a red mist of pure agony as the whip cut into her tender skin. She stiffened in her captors' grip as every muscle in her body clenched against the pain and thin scarlet trails fanned out over her buttocks where the whip bit cruelly into her flesh. She braced herself for yet another blow, passionately determined not to scream as Lavinia paused to trail the whip down her spine and over her hips, so softly it barely touched her. And as she shuddered beneath the vile caress, her traitorous nipples hardened.

'Will you obey me now?' her mistress asked softly.

'Never,' she gasped, and then simply could not stop herself from screaming as the whip swept down again, only this time the pain was even worse as the leather strip sliced into her already burning flesh. The smooth globes of her bottom jerked and quivered beneath the blow, flushing a fiery red as heat radiated through her belly. She groaned, this time from a sick pleasure as she felt her sex moistening helplessly.

Lavinia smiled, and abruptly thrust the handle of the whip between Branna's thighs, rubbing it tantalisingly against her moist cleft. 'Ready yet?' she whispered.

Biting her lip, Branna shook her head.

'Stubborn little bitch!' Lavinia finally snapped and lost her temper completely. 'You will obey me!'

The whip rose and fell and Branna screamed again and again, her pride all but forgotten as her world became a blinding mist of unbearable agony mixed with a perversely deepening pleasure she could not make sense of. Nothing existed except the hot torment, and the corresponding excitement, flaring through her body. 'No more, please!' she heard herself cry. 'No more! I'll do as you say!'

Lavinia stepped back, a cruel smile of satisfaction twisting her heavily painted lips. 'Good,' she panted, 'then you will obey me.'

Calla and Flaminia let go of her, and Branna sank weakly to her knees in front of the Nubian slave. His cock was even more rampant now; watching her being beaten had obviously excited him. With a groan of satisfaction he gripped her hair and pulled her face towards him. Her lips parted, and he quickly slipped his erection into her mouth, grunting with pleasure as the warm wetness engulfed him. She gagged at first, but as her saliva and his seeping semen soon lubricated him, it became easier to swallow his engorged shaft, and her own excitement began to mount as she sucked him. Her tongue swirled around his swollen glans, and her head bobbed rhythmically back and forth as she took more and more of the big black erection into her mouth. Squirming, she rubbed her breasts against his toned thighs like a cat in heat, her nipples tight and hard against his smooth skin. From the corner of her eye she could see Lavinia seated on the couch avidly watching her performance, her own mouth slack with lust. Calla stood behind her, her hands hidden inside her mistress's *stola* as she caressed the sagging breasts there. Lavinia's skirts were pulled up around her waist, and Flaminia's face was buried between her heavy thighs.

The sight should have disgusted Branna, yet it only served to intensify her excitement, and her head moved faster as she sucked the Nubian's impressive cock. Cradling his heavy balls in one hand, she remembered what she had done for Cerdoc once and reached around his buttocks to slide a daring finger into his tight anus. The cock between her lips promptly swelled to huge dimensions, and burst, spurting hot seed against the roof of her mouth and onto her tongue. She swallowed every last drop, moaning with pleasure as her own orgasm irresistibly followed his, while a cry from across the room revealed their mistress was also reaching the peak of her lust and climaxing along with her slaves.

Panting, Branna slid to the floor, the black youth's warm white milk trickling from the corners of her mouth. Shame overwhelmed her. Not only had Lavinia beaten her and forced her to do her will, she had actually enjoyed it.

'Now you are truly my slave,' her mistress said, smiling down at her, and Branna's humiliation was complete.

Later that evening, when Branna and Calla were in the kitchen together fetching food and wine for Lavinia, the back door to the *culina* opened and a tall man entered. His tunic was grimy and he was covered from head to toe in the dust of long travel. All eyes turned towards him as he limped wearily towards the table, poured himself a beaker of wine, and gulped it down.

'That's better,' he said with relief. 'I've been riding since daylight. I don't know which is stiffer, the horse or me.' He reached for the wine jug again, but Clovis's hand came firmly down on top of it.

'Stop your blathering and get to the point,' the cook demanded. 'We're not interested in how sore your arse is. What news do you bring?'

The man looked up and grinned, his teeth a startling white against his sunburnt skin. 'Well,' he drawled, 'since you ask so nicely, I might just tell you, provided I get another beaker of that fine Falerian grape juice.'

Muttering sourly, Clovis poured him one.

The messenger drank it down and smacked his lips appreciatively. 'The master will be here by tomorrow afternoon,' he announced, grinning at Clovis again. 'So you'd better get that fat backside of yours moving, if you know what's good for you. He'll expect a decent meal when he arrives.' He began beating the dust from his clothes. 'And now, if you don't mind, I'd better make myself presentable and go and tell the mistress the good news,' and with a jaunty wave he sauntered out of the kitchen.

'Get up,' hissed Chloe, shaking Branna violently. 'The mistress is running mad. You are to attend her immediately.'

Branna groaned, swung her aching legs over the side of the bed, and yawned prodigiously. Washing her hands and face as quickly as possible, she pulled on her tunic and twisted her hair into a knot at the nape of her neck. Satisfied she at least looked presentable, she hurried into the main house and along the corridor to her mistress's room.

Chloe's description had been accurate; Lavinia was pacing her room like a caged wolf. The couch was piled high with rejected clothing, and a red handprint on Calla's cheek indicated she had already fallen foul of her mistress's ill temper.

'About time, too!' she snapped, turning on Branna. 'Go and run my bath and fetch milk from the *culina* to add to the water. It will soften my skin.'

Branna hurried away to do her bidding, much to Clovis's disapproval as he saw his supplies sacrificed on the altar of Lavinia's vanity.

In the *latrina* Branna stared around her in bewilderment. This was the first time she had entered this room alone, which was reserved for family and guests when it was inconvenient to attend the public baths. She and her fellow slaves used a more basic amenity - a wooden toilet with a keyhole-shaped seat - but this room was far more luxurious. The walls were covered with mosaics of fish, there was a sink as well as a toilet, and a small bathing pool with steps leading down into it formed the centre of the luxurious space.

She poured the milk into the pool, and fiddled with the small metal wheels that apparently controlled the water. There was a gurgling sound, and water did begin gushing out of two holes inside the pool.

She had barely finished adjusting the temperature when Lavinia appeared with Calla and Flaminia scuttling behind her. They helped the matron out of her robe, and assisted her as she descended into the pool, where she lay back spread-eagled in the warm, milk-clouded water.

But if her slaves thought the relaxing bath would sweeten their mistress's temper, they were sadly mistaken. By the time Lavinia had been patted dry, they had all felt the pain of her displeasure. Branna received a buffet to the ear for her clumsiness, and Flaminia's cheek was as red and puffy as Calla's, the result of a spiteful slap from a wet hand.

Back in her room, their surly mistress seated herself in front of her mirror. 'Fetch my cosmetics,' she commanded.

As Calla and Flaminia worked to achieve the impossible and make Lavinia young and beautiful again, the inexperienced Branna was relegated to holding the various pots and tiny plates the cosmetics were mixed on, and she watched in fascination as the transformation began. First a layer of powdered chalk was applied to Lavinia's face that turned it as white as the marble statues in the forum. Then red ochre gave colour to her cheeks and lips, saffron stained her eyelids, and finally antimony darkened her eyebrows and eyelashes. Judging by Lavinia's smug smile as she turned her head from side to side admiring the results, she was pleased by her appearance, but to Branna she looked like a gilded corpse.

'Put on my jewellery,' Lavinia instructed a little more mildly, and Calla quickly slipped long golden earrings into her mistress's pierced earlobes, adjusted a heavy necklace of gold and turquoise around her neck, and slipped half-a-dozen bangles onto each one of her wrists. 'Now fetch my wig,' she told Flaminia, and Branna stared in amazement as the other girl brought it out. Coiled and elaborately braided, it was the shade of red-gold so admired by Roman matrons, and she wondered what unfortunate slave had been shorn to adorn her mistress. Calla drew Lavinia's own hair into a tight knot, and Flaminia gingerly placed the wig on her head, tugging it gently into place so all traces of the real greying hair were concealed.

'Excellent,' Lavinia simpered coyly into the mirror. 'Now bring me my best *stola*, the one with the gold embroidery around the hem.'

In the end, Lavinia was a ghastly parody of youth and beauty. The powdered chalk had already settled into the crow's feet around her eyes and into the grooves of discontent alongside her mouth, while the soft red-gold hair served only to draw attention to the hard middle-aged face beneath it. All the cosmetics in the world could not hide the damage done not so much by the passage of time as by the woman's own ill nature. Thankfully, she was unaware of her slaves' thoughts, and she was actually smiling as she ordered them to fetch her some food. 'Oh, and bring a jug of wine, too,' she added. 'I shall drink a toast to my husband and his safe return.'

But as the day dragged on, and there was still no sign of Marcus Cornelius, Lavinia became increasingly impatient. She merely picked at her food as she drained the wine-jug again, and again. Her carefully applied cosmetics had began to run as she perspired, leaving black streaks beneath her eyes, and her golden wig was askew, revealing a handful of grey hairs beneath it.

By late afternoon she was hopelessly drunk and looked like a raddled whore after a busy night. 'Fetch me more wine,' she slurred, staring at her slaves with bleary eyes. 'I want more wine.'

'And perhaps a little bread and cheese, mistress?' Calla suggested tentatively.

Lavinia glared at her and raised a hand to slap her again, but her senses were so befuddled that she missed her target. 'I said wine!' she screeched. 'Do as you are told, or it will be the worse for you.'

Exchanging a hopeless glance with the other girls, Calla hurried off to the *culina*. She had just returned when there was the hail of a distant trumpet, followed by the sound of scurrying feet.

'The master!' Flaminia exclaimed with relief. 'Mistress, the master has returned!'

'Fetch me my *pallium*,' Lavinia muttered, 'I shall greet him at the gate.' She stumbled to her feet and waited, swaying slightly, while they brought her cloak and draped it around her shoulders. Walking with exaggerated care she then made her way out of the house and down to the gate to await the arrival of her husband. The whole household seemed to have gathered there already, ranged in order of rank from Fabius down to the lowliest kitchen slave. Branna took her place behind her mistress, and craned her neck to catch the first glimpse of her master.

The entourage was small compared with that of some nobles - a mere twenty or so slaves and attendants running alongside a litter. Marcus Cornelius rode at the head of the procession, and at the sight of him Branna's throat went dry as for one heart-stopping moment his broad shoulders and lean body reminded her painfully of Cerdoc. She swallowed her emotions, and when she looked more closely, the resemblance vanished. Although he had the same build and ease of carriage, his hair was dark and greying at the temples, and his eyes were brown, not blue. Cerdoc's nose had been straight, whereas this man's nose had been broken in some past battle and set rather crookedly, although he was handsome enough to bear the slight deformity with dignity.

He swung himself easily out of the saddle, and strode towards his wife. 'Greetings, Lavinia,' he said formally.

Lavinia flung herself unceremoniously into his arms. 'Oh, Marcus, Marcus!' she sobbed, clutching him feverishly. 'I've missed you so much!'

He disentangled himself from her grasping fingers, and pushed her gently away from him. His tunic was smeared with her cosmetics, and Branna noticed the fleeting grimace of distaste that crossed his face. Behind him the curtains of the litter parted and a woman stepped out, followed by a small child. Branna's eyes widened. It was like seeing herself in a distorting mirror. The girl was taller than she was and her hair was fairer, but apart from that they could easily have been sisters.

Suddenly Lavinia turned from a sobbing wife to a raging virago. 'You bastard!' she shrieked, kicking at him. 'How dare you bring your whore into my house?'

'You forget yourself, wife,' he said coldly. 'I am the master of this house, and I do what I please.' He turned towards her personal slaves, and his eyes lingered on Branna for a brief moment. 'Your mistress is unwell,' he told them. 'Take her away and attend to her. I shall wait upon her after I have dined.'

Obediently, Lavinia's slaves led the cowed and weeping woman back to her room, where she collapsed across her couch and sobbed herself into a drunken stupor.

CHAPTER 5

As it turned out, the master of the house did not visit his wife that night. The laundry slave was agog with the news the following morning as he carried the sheets to the boiler. 'Not much point in washing 'em,' he grinned. 'They've not seen much action.'

'Couldn't raise the standard, eh?' Clovis remarked, smirking. 'I'm not surprised he couldn't get a hard-on. You can take a horse to water, but you can't make it drink.' He sniggered. 'Mind you, that's not going to put her ladyship in a very good mood.' He winked at Lavinia's three slaves. 'I wouldn't fancy being in your sandals this morning.'

It was a very subdued trio that made its way to their mistress's room. The gods only knew what sort of treatment they would receive today.

Lavinia did not even notice their arrival. She was seated before her mirror, her eyes glittering dangerously. 'I'll show him,' she muttered. 'Spurn me for that trollop, would he? Well, what he can do, I can do.' She suddenly realised her girls had arrived and turned towards them with a terrifying smile. There was madness behind it - madness and cruelty.

'Ah, the Iceni wench,' she said slowly, menacingly. 'I have a little treat in store for you. This afternoon, when my husband is at the forum, you and I are going to enjoy ourselves. Well, at least *I* shall enjoy myself.'

Branna's blood turned to ice.

'Now make me beautiful, quickly,' the woman snapped.

Three times Calla and Flaminia layered Lavinia's face with cosmetics, and three times she made them clean it off and begin all over again, and always the wineglass was at her hand. Eventually she was grudgingly satisfied with the results. 'Now fetch my midday meal,' she said, waving them away. 'Then you may eat yourselves.'

As they walked past Marcus Cornelius's *tablinium on the way to the culina*, Branna heard his voice, followed by a woman's low, throaty laugh. Whatever the master was doing in his study, she did not think he was reading scrolls.

When they returned to their mistress's room, Lavinia was reclining on her couch and accepted the food with an imperious nod. 'You may leave me now,' she said haughtily, 'except for you, my little Iceni.'

'Did you think I would renege on my promise?' she went on when the other two had gone. 'Return here as soon as you have eaten. You will accompany me this afternoon.'

Back in the *culina*, Branna's churning stomach rebelled against the sight of food. She picked at the bread on her plate, reducing it to a pile of crumbs as her mind ran riot trying to imagine what Lavinia had in store for her. Pushing her plate away she drew a deep breath, got to her feet, and walked leadenly back to her mistress's room.

Lavinia was waiting for her. 'Bring me my *pallium*,' she said. 'I have ordered Tamba to fetch a litter. It will be here soon.'

As if on cue, the black slave who guarded the door hurried in. 'Your litter, mistress,' he said, bowing awkwardly. He cast a sideways glance at Branna, and his tongue darted out to lick his lips in a suggestive fashion that made her face burn with shame. 'You want I come with you, mistress?' he asked hopefully. His face fell at her refusal, but he shrugged philosophically and ushered Lavinia out to the waiting litter.

Fabius was there, and he helped his mistress in before taking his place beside it. Settling herself comfortably amongst the cushions, Lavinia waved to indicate she was ready. Four burly men lifted the mobile couch, and set off at a brisk pace while Branna hurried alongside it, hard-pressed to keep up with Fabius's long stride. It was not until after they had threaded their way through the busy traffic at the heart of Rome that it dawned on her that half the city seemed to be heading in the same direction as they were.

Branna heard the noise before they reached their destination, a dull roar issuing from thousands of throats. Then they crested a hill and she discerned its source - the Circus Maximus, the greatest amphitheatre in Rome. It sprawled massively over the flat plain, a huge edifice dedicated to the Roman love of entertainment. Hordes of people, rich and poor alike, were streaming through the many entrances, some of them looking as if they had queued overnight judging by their tired and dishevelled appearance.

And the closer they got, the worse the crowd became. Lavinia tutted impatiently, holding a perfumed cloth to her nose against the smell of sweat and dirt emanating from the masses. Her litter-bearers pushed people ruthlessly aside and eventually reached an entrance, where Fabius helped his mistress alight. He walked ahead, keeping the riff-raff at bay with his staff, while Branna followed behind Lavinia, staring around in fascination. The long walkway was packed with food vendors peddling their various wares, and with whores vying with each other to attract the attention of the passers-by.

Lavinia ignored everyone. Her head held high she strutted forward, secure in her position. Not for her the interminable queues or the fight for a seat; she took her place by noble right in one of the coveted front rows, settling herself comfortably before dismissing Fabius.

Branna knelt at her feet and fanned her. From her position she could see the whole of the great arena. Although the emperor's dais itself was empty, it seemed the rest of the city was present. Around her rose tier upon tier of seats, all of them packed to bursting with the citizens of Rome. It was a spectacle in itself, and the sound of thousands of voices was like a great ocean beating on the shore of her skull. Yet it was nothing to the noise that issued when the gates opened, and the first contestants made their way out onto the sand. Branna shuddered then and wished she could cover her ears, for it was as if a great beast had opened its maw and roared its greed and hunger at the universe.

The two men in the arena circled each other warily. One was armed with a net and a trident, while the other held a knife and a short stabbing sword. They lunged and parried, sweat glistening on their bodies beneath the merciless sun. There was a long, indrawn breath as the sword-bearer caught the other man on the arm, slashing his flesh open from shoulder to wrist. He had drawn first blood and his face split in a triumphant grin.

But his triumph was short-lived.

As he advanced for the kill his opponent threw his net. It spun through the air and settled over him, hopelessly entangling him. His efforts to free himself only served to enmesh him further, his weapon useless in the clinging web, and as he fought against it the other man danced round him and stabbed repeatedly with the trident. Scarlet flowers bloomed against his brown skin, and his struggles gradually weakened. Finally he staggered and fell, and a great roar of bloodlust issued from the crowd.

'Kill him! Kill him! Kill him!'

Breathing heavily but smiling maliciously, the victor stooped down, fumbled beneath the folds of the net, and straightened up again holding his vanquished opponent's sword. He flourished it in the air, bent over again, and pulling the net away promptly disembowelled the man on the ground. Then arena slaves ran out and dragged the corpse away by the heels, leaving a glistening trail of blood that yet more slaves hurried to cover up with fresh sand. Still smiling manically the victor followed them out, bowing to the cheering crowd.

The young Iceni woman looked at the Romans around her. Their eyes glinted avidly as they chatted with each other between bouts, eating and drinking as they discussed the points of the last fight. One highborn lady had her hand beneath her *stola* and was fingering herself, her mouth open as she panted in excitement.

Sickened by the sight, Branna closed her eyes for a moment. This was not civilisation. A man had just died for their entertainment, and they were laughing and stuffing their faces with sweetmeats. These people were no better than beasts, and like beasts, they were already hungry for more blood.

And so it went on, an endless stream of death and pain and horror throughout the long afternoon, until Branna's senses reeled with the stench of blood hanging heavily in the hot air, and she could practically taste it in the back of her mouth. Her head ached and she kept her eyes closed much of the time to shut out the gruesome spectacle, her face pale and drawn from the effort she made to stop herself being sick all over her mistress's sandaled feet.

At one point a hand gripped her hair and jerked her head back savagely. 'What?' Lavinia sneered down at her. 'Is the entertainment too strong for our little warrior maiden's stomach? I had not thought you barbarians so lily-livered.'

Branna stared at her mistress in disgust. 'In my land we die for a cause, not for the titillation of an unwashed mob, or the perverted pleasure of pampered bitches like you.'

The blow that immediately followed the heartfelt insult flung her head sideways and made her ears ring, but she continued to glare at Lavinia in silent defiance even as a kick in the ribs followed the vicious slap.

'Go and find me a litter,' Lavinia commanded. 'And do it now!'

Branna got eagerly to her feet, fought her way through other overweight matrons, and hurried down the walkway. A whore was servicing a client in one of the alcoves, her tunic bunched around her waist, moaning in mock passion as the man pumped and ground himself between her thighs. Utterly sickened by the whole debauched environment Branna averted her eyes and quickened her pace.

She quickly secured a litter and ran back to inform Lavinia, who smiled, and graciously bade her friends farewell before sauntering ahead of Branna, who was left to gather up the fan and perfume bottle and various other paraphernalia the woman had left strewn around her seat.

'Shall I tell them to carry you home, mistress?' Branna enquired once Lavinia had settled herself comfortably amongst the cushions of the litter.

'Home?' echoed Lavinia with a mocking laugh. 'Of course not.' She smiled at Branna, her eyes alight with cruel amusement. 'The entertainment has only just begun...

'Move!' she ordered the litter bearers. 'To the *subura!*'

Branna followed apprehensively just behind the litter as it set off. But instead of passing through the busy centre of the city and heading uphill towards the villa, they turned deeper into a labyrinth of streets, into an area she had never been before. And the further they went, the seedier the neighbourhood became. The road narrowed as more and more stalls grew up on either side of it, selling everything from second-hand clothing to scrawny chickens squawking inside wicker baskets. Houses and tenements crowded together, shutting out fresh air and light, and over everything hung the stench of dirt and poverty.

The smell of cheap meat frying on the cook-stalls made Branna feel sick, but what astonished her most were the people themselves. If the centre of the city was crowded, this place teemed like an anthill. Dirty, shabbily dressed citizens rubbed shoulders with the gilded youth of the city, their wealth made obvious by their pristine togas, fat purses and contented expressions. The contrast between them and the inhabitants of this down-at-heel area was brutally stark, yet everyone seemed to accept it as a matter of course. Even the passage of Lavinia's litter aroused little interest.

Then Branna realised that every other house was either a tavern or a brothel. She stared open-mouthed at the rampant phallus carved above the lintel of a doorway to indicate the kind of service the house provided. Even as she watched, the door swung open and a drunk was forcefully evicted, immediately followed by a deftly flung pot that bounced off his skull. A painted prostitute stood on the threshold screaming obscenities at her former client. 'And don't show your face here again, you fucking whoreson!' She slammed the door behind her. The man staggered around, blood streaming down his face from the wound in his scalp where the pot had struck him, but no one in the laughing crowd rushed to his assistance. Lavinia's litter simply swerved around him, and when Branna glanced back over her shoulder he was lying unconscious in the street with several ragged children picking over his unconscious body like little carrion crows.

As the road continued to narrow the surroundings became increasingly squalid, and Branna seriously began to wonder what Lavinia was doing in this part of the city. Why, in the name of all the gods, would a fine lady lower herself by coming to such a place as this?

The litter finally drew to a halt outside a rundown house, and Lavinia descended, pulling the hood of her *pallium* over her head to hide her face. Paying the bearers, she dismissed them, turned towards the door, and banged on it imperiously.

For a few moments nothing happened, and then Branna's sharp ears caught the sound of shuffling feet. The door creaked open, and a suspicious face peered out at them. Like an evil caricature carved from some gnarled and ancient tree, all humanity had been leached from the countenance regarding them with smouldering eyes, in which the only emotions were lust and greed. She could not even tell if the creature was male or female so little personality did it possess; it looked more like an evil woodland nymph than a person.

At the sight of Lavinia the apparition twisted its face into what passed for a welcoming smile, and pulled the door wide. 'My lady,' it croaked. 'You honour us with your presence.'

'Thank you, Haephestus,' Lavinia replied civilly. She entered the house, and a reluctant Branna followed behind her. A small leather bag exchanged hands, clinking gently as it passed from the matron's pampered fingers to the creature's bony hand.

Inside the house was dark and empty; smelling of age and neglect, and no matter how hard she tried Branna could come up with no reason why the fastidious Lavinia would wish to visit such a place. Perhaps an ancient Sybil lived here and her mistress wished to have her future foreseen.

'Come this way, my lady,' their evil-looking host said in a croaking voice that still failed to give away its sex. Turning, it led the way, moving with surprising speed and agility considering its stooped posture. They walked deeper into the house, their footsteps echoing through the empty rooms. Finally the gnome-like figure stopped before a blank wall in which a single torch burned, its flames casting distorting shadows over their faces.

Branna stared at him in anxious bewilderment. Were they expected to drift through the wall like spirits of the dead? Then she noticed the heavy ring set in one of the marble slabs. It looked as if it had been there since the beginning of time, yet when the creature tugged on it, it moved with well-oiled ease. Branna took a forced step back, and stared with trepidation at the uneven stone steps leading down into a yawning, chilly darkness.

Then, reaching for the torch, their host plucked it from the wall and held it above his head. Wild shadows flickered across his face, making him look even more demonic.

Lavinia smiled, and her teeth gleamed in the reddish darkness like those of a she-wolf after a bloody feast. 'Oh no you don't!' she hissed, grabbing her slave's arm as Branna instinctively backed away another unsteady step.

The squat little man began hobbling down the steps, and Branna was forced to descend behind him. She reached out a hand to steady herself, but then snatched it back again as it came into contact with the wall's slimy surface. Below her she heard a muffled scream, followed by the sound of hysterical laughter, and her blood went cold.

At the bottom of the steps they followed a narrow passage, ending in another seemingly blank wall. Holding the torch high Haephestus fumbled at an obscene carving, and the wall swung slowly back with a deep, ominous grinding sound. Dazzled by the sudden light, it took Branna's eyes a few moments to adjust, and when they did she gasped at the sight before her. She was looking into a large underground room, apparently running the full length of the empty house above it. Oil lamps hung from the ceiling, their flames illuminating a scene straight from the underworld. Tapestries embroidered in sparkling gold and silver thread draped the walls, and statues engaged in every sexual position known to man and beast adorned shallow niches, the lamplight flickering over them making it seem as if their marble and ebony limbs were moving.

Low and ornately carved couches were arranged along the walls, the tables in front of them strewn with food and beakers of wine. And on the couches sprawled men and women in various attitudes of abandon, their faces leering masks of debauchery. Two naked girls knelt before a fat-bellied man, one girl dripping wine over his erection while the other girl lapped it off with her tongue, her head bobbing back and forth in his lap as she took his full length and girth between her lips.

Branna looked away, only to see a respectable elderly matron throw her head back in ecstasy as a man young enough to be her grandson plunged his face between her skeletal thighs.

Sick at heart, the young Iceni kept turning her head away, but there was no relief. In the centre of the room was a slightly raised dais where a naked girl, her body oiled and glistening in the torchlight, writhed sensuously to the sound of pipes and lyres while a python coiled itself around her waist and shoulders. As Branna watched in horror, the snake slithered down over the girl's buttocks and between her legs, its tongue flickering obscenely as its head emerged from between the lips of her sex like some grotesque phallus. Her hips pumping sensuously and she caressed the reptile, moaning in pleasure as the smooth, firm body rubbed against her vulva. Beads of perspiration stood out like jewels on her oiled skin, her legs trembled as she shrieked her release, and a handful of coins were flung at her feet.

Then suddenly two expressionless male slaves clothed in nothing but skimpy loincloths stepped up behind Branna and gripped both her arms. She was dragged struggling across the room, through a curtained doorway, and the last thing she saw was Lavinia clicking her fingers at a naked slave boy, who responded obediently to her summons and was shamelessly fondled until quickly fully aroused, then the curtain swung back into place behind her, obscuring the vision of depravity.

As soon as the male slaves released Branna she made a break for the nearest doorway, but a cynical voice drew her up short. 'Don't waste your time, sweetheart.' The snake-girl was sitting naked and cross-legged on the floor counting her coins, her pet python curled harmlessly up in a basket beside her. She gave Branna a twisted smile. 'Nothing that bunch of perverted bastards would enjoy better than chasing down a screaming girl, and when they caught you...' She closed her eyes and shuddered dramatically. 'Best just do as you're told - at least that way you'll get out of here in one piece.'

'B-but, what are they going to do to me?'

The girl rolled her eyes. 'Whatever they like,' she replied. She rose to her feet in one graceful motion, reached for the collar around Branna's neck, and fingered it gently. 'This gives them the right to you, body and soul. Don't you know that by now?' Her hand went to her own unadorned neck. 'At least I'm a free agent.' She laughed softly and bitterly. 'Free to starve, no doubt, once my looks are gone, but for now I do whatever I can to get by, and if that means fondling a serpent while those perverts watch, then so be it.' She slipped into her tunic, put on her cloak and picked up her basket, leaning slightly to one side against its weight. 'Good luck,' she said, and with a pitying smile parted some curtains and disappeared.

Branna was looking around the small, whitewashed room when Haephestus walked in flanked by the two slave boys who had escorted her there. The obsequious smile he put on for Lavinia's benefit had disappeared, leaving only a cruel smirk in its wake. She backed away from him until her shoulders touched the wall and she could go no further. 'W-what do you want from me?' she asked in a quavering voice.

The squat figure's lip curled as if the question was too stupid to even deserve an answer. 'Strip off your clothes,' he ordered, flinging something at her.

Branna caught the garment, and stared down at it with blank incomprehension. She was holding two pieces of soft black leather she had no idea what to do with.

'Put them on,' Haephestus snapped impatiently. 'We don't have all day. My clients are waiting.'

'Never!' she hissed, letting the skimpy garment drop to the floor.

'Please yourself,' he said, shrugging. 'You will obey me in the end. They all do.' He clicked his fingers and the two male slaves moved towards her again. Leering with pleasure at their task, they ripped the tunic from her trembling body while Haephestus stood by grinning as they fondled her roughly.

Branna had no option now but to pick up the black leather garments if she did not wish to remain naked. Her face red with shame and loathing, she wriggled into them, and much to her horror she discovered that instead of concealing her nudity the flimsy leather merely served to enhance it. The tight-fitting lower garment was so cunningly cut that it did not cover her bottom at all. The thong bisecting her buttocks drew attention to their smooth white curves, and the way it was split open in front made it dig so deeply into her labia that her *mons veneris* bulged enticingly, the lips of her sex pulled apart to give tantalising glimpses of the glistening rosy succulence within.

The band around her bosom was equally revealing. Her breasts were crushed together, their creamy whiteness spilling over the top, while her nipples, forced into erectness, poked through holes cut strategically into the leather. She could hardly breathe, and when she did the garment bit into her cruelly, making her even more conscious of how soft and vulnerable her flesh was.

Haephestus stood back and smirked wickedly, obviously revelling in her wide

61

frightened eyes and trembling lips. The black leather stood out in startling contrast to her pale skin, and how tightly it fitted made her look like a victim trussed for sacrifice. He reached into the evil-smelling folds of his robe, and produced a length of black cloth he handed to one of his slaves. 'Cover her eyes,' he said.

Branna flinched away, but it was useless. As one man held her the other one covered her eyes with the blindfold. Then her arms were seized and pulled in front of her, and she felt the rough caress of a rope against her skin. She winced as her wrists were bound tightly together, and then someone picked up the trailing end of the rope and tugged on it, forcing her to follow behind him or fall on her face. Whimpering, she stumbled forwards. Her blindness seemed to hone her other senses to unnatural sharpness, and she shivered as she felt the curtain brush against her flanks as they passed through the doorway.

She felt the warm air of the main room waft over her, and she could smell the burning oil and heavy perfumes barely masking the reek of perspiration and sex. Worse still were the noises, all the grunting and moaning, and the slap of flesh against flesh accompanied by obscene, wet sucking sounds.

And yet the silence that fell as she entered the room was infinitely more terrifying than anything else. It was as if some monstrous creature had ceased slobbering for a moment to look up from the meat it was devouring at the smell of fresh young prey. Her skin prickled and dread stiffened her back, along with something even worse... a perverse anticipation. Her mind completely rejected what was about to happen, but her body was betraying her yet again. The swollen lips of her sex chafed against each other as she walked, sending delicious sensations coursing through her pelvis, and her nipples were almost painfully stiff. She groaned in shame, but there was no doubt about the fact that her pussy was very wet.

She was yanked to an abrupt halt, she heard the sound of a rope hissing through the air, and then she screamed as her arms were hauled upwards. Her wrists were secured, and suddenly she was dangling from the ceiling like a carcase in a butcher's shop. She panted from the strain as every muscle in her body was stretched to the limit, and tried desperately to see through or beneath the blindfold, but there was only an impenetrable darkness before her. The blood pounded through her heart and in her temples as she waited... and waited...

Her ears caught a thin whistling sound, and she shrieked in agony as the whip cut across her exposed flesh, making her buttocks jump and quiver. Her whole body jerked on the rope as the lash curled around her hips, leaving a trail of fire behind it. There was a long pause - long enough for her to begin to hope the first blow had also been the last - before she heard the awful hissing sound again and the second lash bit into her flesh. She screamed and jerked violently on the end of the rope, straining to put some of her weight on the tips of her toes, her thigh muscles quivering with the effort. Yet she could feel her nipples jutting full and hard through the holes in the constraining breast-band, betraying her excitement. Every inch of her body strained in fear of the next kiss of the lash... fear and expectation.

Another blow fell and she screamed as the pain came again, bringing a dreadful pleasure in its wake. Her pussy throbbed and moistened as heat coursed through her belly, and she became oblivious to everything except the exquisite agony. Again and again the lash curled around her hips and left its vicious mark, until the pale skin of her bottom was a fiery red. She lost count of the blows as her cries of protest gradually turned to whimpers of desire. Like a beaten bitch she yearned only to crawl on her belly and lick the hand that held the whip.

When the ordeal finally ended she hung motionless from her bonds, her breath coming in ragged gasps, lost in the conflicting sensations raging through her flesh. Time seemed to stretch out to infinity... and then she felt the soft brush of a woman's breasts against her own. The nipples pressed against hers, and then long hair tickled her skin as a head bent to suckle them. She whimpered again as teeth grazed her delicate flesh, and moaned as a gentle hand caressed the insides of her thighs, stroking the soft flesh before parting the lips of her vulva to slip a finger into her wet, hot pussy. The finger began to move, slowly at first, then more and more quickly, and against her will Branna felt the muscles of her thighs slacken to allow it easier access. Giving herself up to the pleasure pulsing through her she flung back her head, and the blindfold slipped off. For a moment she could see nothing, and then her eyes adjusted to the light and she found herself looking, not at another woman like herself, but at a loathsome freak of nature.

She cried out again, this time in horror at the thing that had its hands on her. Long hair framed a debauched androgynous face, and the body below it was like that of some dreadful creature from mythology. Above the waist the being was female, with heavy, swinging breasts, but below the waist it was all male, with an enormous swollen cock jutting from the base of its hairy belly, beads of semen seeping from its bulbous purple tip. She made an effort to cringe away from the thing mauling her, but the rope bit into her wrists and held her in place.

Smiling lopsidedly at her futile attempts to struggle free, the creature slipped its arms around her hips and dragged her even closer. Its flabby dugs crushed her own firm breasts as it ground itself against her, its thick member pushing its way between her slender thighs. Abandoning all pretence at gentleness, it dug the fingers of one hand cruelly into Branna's flesh as it pulled open the lips of her sex with the other. She whimpered pitifully as its hips jerked forward, and its monstrous erection eased and stretched its way inside her.

It pulled out, only to plunge in deep again, and it fucked her swiftly and aggressively, making her breasts quiver with each thrust. Branna groaned with unwanted pleasure as the base of the creature's cock rutted against the nub of her clitoris, and its heavy balls swung deliciously against her vulva. Closing her eyes in order not to see the hideous face, she imagined it was Cerdoc penetrating her. Her body might be trapped, but her mind was free... she was not being fucked by a monster in some subterranean Roman cellar, she was making love to her betrothed...

Her breathing quickened as the turgid cock plunged in and out of her. Her hips writhed as she met each thrust with one of her own, forcing the monstrous phallus even deeper inside her, the pain and heat from her beaten bottom serving only to intensify her ecstasy. Pain and pleasure, pleasure and pain... she could not tell the difference between them any more and she no longer cared. Her mouth open, muscles tense from the effort, she strained towards release, and it was almost within her grasp when the creature pulled out of her abruptly, leaving her teetering on the edge of fulfilment, and she opened her eyes just in time to see the she-male's cock shooting a fountain of spunk all over her belly.

The blindfold was slipped back over her eyes, and Branna whimpered with frustration in the renewed darkness, her body craving satisfaction. Then she cried out as more hands began crawling over her, painfully pinching her taut nipples, sliding down over her belly to caress her wet sex, and parting her cheeks to probe her anus. For a moment she froze in terror wondering just how many of them there were pawing at her, but then she gave herself up to a feral lust.

Another erection penetrated her slick pussy while yet another pierced her agonisingly from behind, its length and girth sinking its way deep between her yielding buttocks. Trapped between two avaricious cocks she moaned in shameless delight as they began thrusting in unison, sending pulses of blissful agony through her pelvis and her ravaged bottom. She lost track of time then, and of the number of hands and mouths and lips and cocks that caressed her, inside and out. Nothing existed except her insatiable greed for more, and more, and more...

When Branna was finally cut free she collapsed to the floor in absolute exhaustion. After a moment she found strength enough to lift the blindfold from over her eyes, and look around her at a ring of flushed, sneering faces. She had no idea which of them had used her, but it had felt like all of them. She shuddered in shame and horror, and then a coin chinked at her feet and made her humiliation complete - it was a reward for her services.

Another followed the first coin, and soon the floor around her was covered with glinting metal. Her lips set grimly as she pushed herself to her knees, and began gathering them up. If she was a whore now, she might as well accept her payment. And as she did so a frail tendril of hope began unfurling inside her soul. Perhaps something could be salvaged from this awful experience after all; she could put the coins away and begin saving for her freedom.

Her determination set, Branna was eagerly picking up the last *sesterces* when a foot kicked her in the ribs.

'I'll take those, thank you,' Lavinia snapped, staring coldly down at her.

'But you can't, they're mine,' Branna protested.

'They're only yours if I permit it.' Her mistress smiled cruelly. 'And I do not permit it. Anything my slave earns or owns belongs to me. Haephestus!'

The twisted little man came shuffling forward, and the coins were prised from Branna's reluctant fingers and handed over to Lavinia, who counted them with satisfaction.

'Hmm, a very profitable afternoon,' she crowed, slipping them into her pouch. 'A very profitable afternoon indeed.' She turned back to Haephestus. 'Now order me a litter and have her dressed and ready before it arrives.'

In the tiny backroom again, Branna struggled out of her black leather costume and tried to wipe away the disgusting evidence of the afternoon's activities and excesses, and then, as she followed the hateful Lavinia from the terrible den of iniquity, she swore by all her gods that one day she would visit revenge upon her.

The journey back to the villa was lost in a mist of exhaustion for Branna, who was scarcely aware of trudging along behind the litter until Lavinia, irritated by her slow pace, called it to a halt and had the bearers pick her up like a sack of grain and flung her into it. She fell into an exhausted doze at her mistress's feet, and the next thing she was aware of was Lavinia's foot prodding her awake.

Reluctantly she climbed slowly out of the litter, the muscles of her shoulders and thighs screaming in protest with her every movement. Then walking as stiffly as an old woman, she followed her mistress into the villa.

It was early evening and all the lamps were lit. Inside the subterranean room of the *subura* she had lost all track of time. Her ordeal seemed to have gone on forever, yet it could only have lasted a matter of hours. The smell of food wafted in from the *culina* and her belly rumbled in response, reminding her how long it had been since her last meal. How easy it was to wish oneself dead and yet how difficult it was to actually die as the body stubbornly insisted on surviving. If only...

Her morbid thoughts were interrupted by the appearance of Marcus Cornelius. 'Good evening, my dear,' he said to Lavinia. 'Dinner is almost ready. Did you enjoy the games?'

A secretive smile touched his wife's lips as she thought of the 'games' she had so recently enjoyed, and she lowered her eyes to hide her sly amusement. 'Yes, husband, I did, thank you.'

'Good,' he said, barely able to conceal his indifference.

Clearly stung by his lack of interest, Lavinia bit her lip and tried again. 'But it has left me weary, so I shall go to my couch early tonight.' She blushed like a coy maiden. 'Will you be joining me?'

His look of distaste was fleeting and quickly masked, but Branna caught it. 'I am afraid not, my dear,' he replied smoothly. 'I shall be working late. I have important matters to attend to.'

A soft giggle made Branna turn her head. Helga was standing in the shadows, and before she turned away she caught the other Iceni's eye, and winked. It was clear exactly what sort of important matters needed the attention of Marcus Cornelius. Branna glanced at her mistress from the corner of her eye, and was pleased to see that Lavinia's smug smile had been wiped from her lips. Her face was now flushed with suppressed fury at being so openly rejected in favour of a common slave. Branna, on the other hand, had to suppress a grin of satisfaction.

Mastering herself with difficulty, Lavinia forced a smile. 'I shall change immediately and attend dinner with you, husband,' she said, clicking her fingers at Branna. 'Come, girl.'

With a quick courteous bob to Marcus Cornelius, Branna followed her mistress.

Once in the privacy of her room, Lavinia gave vent to her true feelings. With a squawk of fury she hefted the wine jug from the table and sent it flying across the room. It shattered against the wall as a bowl joined it, and the smell of wine and crushed fruit filled the chamber.

Branna hurried to kneel and pick up the scattered pieces of broken pottery while her mistress continued to pace up and down like a caged animal, muttering beneath her breath. 'Shall I help you change for dinner, mistress?' she asked as humbly as possible.

Lavinia whirled around and glared at her, and for one horrible moment Branna feared she would attack her with bare hands as Fabius's warning about what would happen if she had the temerity to defend herself rang in her ears. But instead Lavinia controlled herself, though with obvious difficulty. She ran her eyes over Branna, taking in her dishevelled appearance, and her patrician nose wrinkled at the faint scent of perspiration and sex still emanating from her. Then her upper lip curled in supreme contempt. 'I think not,' she said coldly. 'Go and find Calla and Flaminia and send them to me. I shall bathe directly after dinner. Have my bath ready, and then keep out of my sight for the rest of the night.'

With a sigh of relief, Branna left Lavinia to continue her pacing and muttering.

'Be careful,' she warned her friends as they reluctantly prepared to go and attend to their mistress, 'she's in a fury.' She then gathered up some food and devoured it hungrily before hurrying to run Lavinia's bath. The mood the woman was in, it would not do to keep her waiting. She was accustomed to the amazing system by now, and it was not long before the sunken pool was filled with hot water. She added scented oil to it and knelt to stir it in, inhaling the perfumed steam with pleasure. Then a sudden thought struck her, and she smiled to herself as she tiptoed along the corridor and peeked into the *triclinium*.

Marcus Cornelius was stretched out on his couch and eating heartily while Lavinia sat bolt upright in her chair barely nibbling at her food. It was obvious the meal had only just begun, and it would be at least another hour before they were finished, and Lavinia would be there until the bitter end.

Back in the *latrina*, Branna slipped out of her grubby tunic and walked down the marble steps into the bathing pool, gasping as the hot water enveloped her flesh. Then, exhaling a sigh of sheer delight, she slipped beneath the surface for a long moment. Her breasts bobbing, she sat revelling in the caress of the scented ripples, moaning with pleasure as the delicious heat soothed away the stiff aches of her afternoon ordeal.

She would have liked to linger longer, but she did not dare. Scrubbing herself thoroughly she dipped her head beneath the surface of the water again and rinsed out her hair. Then, as she was stepping out of the bath, another thought struck her, and without hesitating she squatted on the bottom step and emptied her bladder.

Afterwards she looked carefully down at the bath. Tendrils of steam still curled over its surface, hiding any sign of her use, and she smiled to herself at the thought of her fine mistress soaking in dirty water. It was a petty but satisfying revenge, and she was still smiling as she wrapped herself in her damp tunic and hurried silently to her room in the slave quarters, back to her private couch and the merciful oblivion of sleep.

Branna did not know how long she slept before a hand shook her awake. She sat bolt upright as fear lanced through her, until she saw Helga bending over her in the darkness holding one finger to her lips to indicate the need for silence. Cradled in her other arm the master's favourite slave held a small, warmly wrapped bundle.

'The master comes to my room tonight,' she whispered. 'May I leave my son with you?'

Branna nodded, and pulled the covers back to accommodate the little boy. He stirred once in his sleep, his long dark eyelashes fluttering against his soft white cheeks, and then he settled down again and snuggled trustingly against her shoulder.

Helga nodded her thanks, and was gone.

Later, when the sounds of passion filtered through the walls, Branna cuddled the child closer, and smiled thinking of Lavinia lying cold and alone in her bed. Perhaps the gods could be just, after all.

CHAPTER 6

Dread of a return to that subterranean room dogged Branna over the following weeks. As she waited upon Lavinia she lived in constant fear of the order to accompany her to the games. Luckily, her apprehension appeared to be unfounded; her mistress seemed to be far too preoccupied with other thoughts. She was constantly muttering beneath her breath when she thought she was alone, and occasionally she smiled to herself with an expression of such sly cunning on her face that it made Branna's blood run cold. Once, when she was carrying fresh linen to her mistress's room, she was almost knocked over by a dirty, shrivelled-up crone who scuttled past her pulling the hood of her cloak up over her head. She stared after the old woman in surprise, wondering what a respectable Roman matron was doing associating with a creature like that in her own home.

'What are you doing here?' Lavinia demanded, quickly concealing a tiny bottle in the folds of her *stola*.

Branna silently indicated the clean linen she was holding.

'Oh, very well,' her mistress snapped, 'but be quick about it. There are important matters that need my attention.'

As she hurried to replace the covers on Lavinia's couch, Branna wondered what 'matters' involved the contents of the small glass phial her mistress had hidden away so quickly.

Two days later, she found out.

She awoke to the sound of groaning and gasping coming from Helga's room. Her first thought was that Marcus Cornelius was paying the beautiful slave another of his nocturnal visits. She had become used to Helga slipping in at night and leaving little Antonius in her bed. But then reaching sleepily to pull the little boy closer, it dawned on her that she was alone.

She sat up, her bewilderment swiftly turning to anxiety. Helga would never keep her child present while the master made love to her. She strained her ears, and fear gripped her as she realised the sounds she was hearing were not moans of passion - but of distress.

She rose and hurried to Helga's room, and her hands flew to her mouth as she stared in horror at the scene before her.

Her eyes wide and unseeing, Helga lay panting and sweating on the couch, her face pale as a spectre's. As Branna watched, her back arched and her mouth wrenched into a grimace of unbearable pain. But worse still was the sight of Antonius's small body lying white and still beside his mother, his tiny hands still clinging to her in death.

'I'll get help!' Branna gasped, whirling around and racing down the corridor to Fabius's room.

He sat up in bed as she flung the door open. 'How dare you?' he roared.

'Please, it's Helga!' Branna blurted. 'She's dying! Fetch a doctor at once, there's no time to waste!' Then grabbing the jug of water from beside his couch, she ran back to Helga's room. She lifted Antonius's feather-light body and placed it gently in his cot. Then she sat down beside Helga and smoothed the wet hair off her perspiring brow. 'It's all right,' she said softly. 'The doctor is coming, and you'll be fine.' She tore a long strip off her tunic, dipped it in the jug of water, and dripped a little moisture between Helga's parched lips before caressing her burning face and neck with the cool, moist cloth. Helga groaned horribly, and her body went into another wracking spasm, knocking Branna's hand away and sending the jug of water flying.

The rest of the slaves had awoken by now and were clustered in the doorway, staring and muttering.

Branna turned on them in a rage. 'Don't just stand there gawking, fetch me some ice!' she screamed.

Clovis commandeered two of the male slaves and they hurried off to do as she demanded. They returned with a pile of ice chippings wrapped in cloth, and seizing it Branna began packing it around Helga's fevered body. Then a small dark man pushed his way through the chattering slaves, and began examining the patient.

'It is not a contagion,' the Greek doctor announced with authority. 'She has eaten something noxious. There is nothing I can do. She has relieved herself already. We can only hope her body has cleared itself sufficiently and that she is strong enough to recover.' He sighed and shook his head. 'Though I very much doubt it.' Then he smiled at Branna approvingly. 'You are already doing all that can be done for her. Clean her up, keep her cool, and try to make her drink. After that, it is in the hands of the gods whether she lives or dies.'

All night Branna sat beside Helga replacing the ice as it melted and sponging her gently. Clovis had tried to remove Antonius's body, but his mother had become conscious long enough to look wildly around for her child, and it seemed a kindness to leave him with her. His tiny body covered by a fresh linen sheet, his eyes closed, he looked as if he was only sleeping.

Helga's convulsions were milder now, but this was only because she was weakening. Her lovely face was shrunk to a skin-covered skull and her eyes were sunk in dark hollows, all her looks gone. Branna sighed. She had seen death before, and it would not be long now.

As the first light of dawn illuminated the black sky in the east, the door flew open and Marcus Cornelius ran into the room. Pushing Branna aside he cradled Helga's body gently in his arms and rocked it back and forth gently. 'Don't leave me,' he begged quietly. 'Please darling, don't leave me!'

Branna looked at him with a lump in her throat. This was not a master with his slave. This was a man who loved a woman.

Helga's eyes flickered open, and she smiled up at her master. One of her hands rose to weakly caress his face, and then fell limply into his lap. A terrible stillness filled the room then, and Branna new her countrywoman was gone.

Marcus looked from the body of his lover to the body of his son, and a groan of agony burst from his throat before his Roman training took over. Laying Helga gently down again, he rose stiffly to his feet and regarded Branna coldly. 'What happened?' he demanded.

'I-I don't know,' she stammered, frightened by the emotions she glimpsed beneath his iron control. 'The doctor said she had eaten something noxious.'

'Or was poisoned.' His mouth set in a grim line as he stalked towards the door. 'And I know by whom.'

Driven by morbid curiosity, Branna followed him. Helga was beyond her help now, beyond anyone's help, but she could bear witness to the end of her bitter story. Perhaps this time Lavinia had gone too far and would pay the price for her wickedness. If so, Branna wished to be there to see it.

She was hard put to keep up with Marcus Cornelius's long, determined strides, however. He had already burst into his wife's chamber before she reached the doorway.

Lavinia was sitting at her vanity, and was turned towards her husband wearing a welcoming smile. 'Marcus,' she said, and then let out a strangled shriek as his hands closed around her throat and he shook her like a cat with a rat in its jaws.

'Bitch!' he hissed through clenched teeth. 'You killed her! It wasn't enough to make her life a misery, you had to take it from her!'

Choking noisily, she clawed frantically at his hands as she tried in vain to shake her head in denial.

'Where did you get the poison?' he demanded. 'Some crone from the *subura?*'

Branna's hand flew to her mouth as she suddenly remembered the old woman who had passed her in the corridor.

Lavinia's struggles were weakening when her husband abruptly flung her away from him in disgust. 'You're not worth it,' he said contemptuously. 'Helga was ten times the woman you'll ever be, and I shall place her ashes in my family mausoleum.'

Scandalised, Lavinia stared at him in outraged disbelief. '*What*, a common slave's ashes? Are you mad?'

'She may have been a slave, but she was the mother of my child,' he replied icily, 'and as such, she deserves respect.'

'*I* am the mother of your child,' the cruel woman argued, the breath rasping back into her lungs.

His lip curled in contempt. 'Oh yes, and what a child,' he said with disdain. 'A poor creature so twisted in mind and body she has to be hidden away like some guilty secret. And what a loving, devoted mother you are who never visits her child from one year's end to the next.' He laughed bitterly. 'I have been doubly blessed!' He thrust his face into hers. 'Helga will be treated in death with the honour she deserved in life, and I will not hear one word more about it.'

Lavinia opened her mouth to protest again, but the look on his face silenced her. She lowered her eyes, still rubbing at the finger marks on her throat.

'Good,' he said softly, 'we are agreed then.' He left the room, and Branna fled back to the safety of her own quarters to mourn for Helga in private.

It was a long, sad day, during which all the slaves went about their duties in subdued silence. Thankfully, Branna was not called upon to attend her mistress. Evidently grateful to still be alive, Lavinia retired to her bed with a warm cloth around her neck and a dose of poppy brew in her belly and was not missed by anyone.

The *pollinctores* came to wash and embalm the two pitiful bodies, placing a coin beneath their tongues so they could pay their way into the underworld, and when night fell a sad procession set out from the villa. Two musicians played their pipes plaintively as the entire household followed the bodies, torches flaming in the darkness to light the way as they wound their way to a hillside just beyond the city where the funeral pyre waited. Helga and her son were laid gently on top of it, and then Marcus Cornelius opened their eyes for the last time. He kissed them both tenderly, closed their eyes again, and gave the order for the pyre to be lit. As the flames took hold and flared up, the dancing light gave a last semblance of rosy life to the bodies, then they disappeared forever as they were consumed in the cleansing fire. Most of the slaves left after that, returning to the villa and their beds, but Branna remained, hovering in the darkness beyond the funeral pyre, before which Marcus Cornelius stood stone-faced, keeping vigil beside his lost loves.

At some point during the night she must have fallen asleep, because when she came to the fire had almost burned out. The last flames were doused with wine, and the ashes gathered and placed reverently inside an urn. As it was handed to Marcus Cornelius his face crumpled and Branna turned away, reluctant to intrude upon his grief. Unnoticed, she fled down the hillside and through the empty early morning streets back to the villa.

For the next few weeks little was seen of the master. He incarcerated himself in his *tablinium*, and meals left at the door were removed almost untouched.

Lavinia also kept to her room, until the marks on her throat and neck disappeared, and then she gradually resumed her round of visits to friends and to the baths. Her temper was more uncertain than ever, her voice shriller, and her tendency to lash out at her slaves was more in evidence than usual. No matter how careful they were, barely a day passed without them feeling the weight of her displeasure. A miasma of gloom hung over the villa, and the slaves walked softly and spoke in low voices. It was as if the household was ruled over by a ghost and a demon.

It was exactly a month after the funeral when Branna was awoken by muffled sounds coming from next door. She sat up slowly. None of the other slaves would go near Helga's old room; it had remained empty since her death. Had they returned from the dead to cry out for justice?

Swallowing hard, she gathered her courage and rose to investigate. There was still a little oil in her lamp, and she picked it up with a trembling hand and ventured out into the corridor, shivering with cold and apprehension but unable to simply lie on her couch and listen. The strange sounds were louder now, and she could make out a voice muttering broken phrases interspersed by an occasional sob. She was hearing a constant litany of grief and loss that made her wonder if Helga's lost spirit was mourning her murdered child.

Holding her breath, Branna slowly pushed the door open. Her heart almost stopped at the sight of the white shape rocking back and forth on the couch, and then her eyes adjusted to the gloom and she saw it was not the spirit of a dead girl before her but a flesh-and-blood being like herself.

It was the master.

The breath hissed out of her lungs in a sigh of relief.

At the sound he stopped rocking and looked up. The light from the lamp she held fell full on his face, so to him she was only a shadow standing in the doorway. 'Helga?' he whispered, and the expression of joyful hope on his face was heartbreaking.

'No, it is not Helga, master,' she said reluctantly. 'It is Branna. I heard noises and came to see what was making them.' She curtsied briefly. 'Is there anything I can fetch you?'

'The only things I want are beyond fetching,' he answered bitterly. 'Can you go to the underworld and bring back Helga and my son?'

She shook her head sadly.

He put his own head in his hands and groaned. 'I must be going mad,' he muttered. 'Did I really think my grief could call them back from their grave?'

'Or let you join them there?' she added softly. His distress was so touching that for a moment she forgot the vast difference in their social positions. Putting down the lamp, she sat beside him and took his hand. He looked at her, startled, and she smiled wistfully. 'I was not always a slave,' she said. 'I, too, was free to love once, and be loved.' She sighed. 'When my betrothed was killed, my only wish was to die.'

'Poor little Iceni,' he said with rough sympathy. 'So young to lose so much.' Then his mind returned to his own loss, and his hand clutched hers with such force that she winced. 'Helga was young, too. She had her whole life ahead of her. I thought we would grow old together. And my son...' his voice caught. 'My son!' He broke into the harsh wracking sobs of someone who has kept their grief under control for so long they must either let it free, or go mad.

She slipped an arm around his shoulders, pulled his head down against her breasts, and rocked him as gently as if he were a child. 'Shush,' she comforted. 'It will pass. Everything passes.'

Later she could not remember at what point his mouth came down on hers and his clinging arms became a passionate embrace. She could not say exactly when comfort turned to desire. All she knew was that his lips were suddenly parting hers and his hands were fervently exploring her body. He caressed her breasts, kneading their soft fullness before finding their sensitive tips, and running his thumbs around and around them, until she whimpered with pleasure.

Then she moaned as he lowered his head and teased her nipples with his tongue while one of his hands slipped between her thighs and urgently stroked the taut, silken skin of her vulva, until she relaxed and allowed his fingers to slide higher and deeper. It was his turn to moan as he parted the soft lips of her labia and found the hot wetness within as her own hands slid beneath his tunic to explore his muscled body. She toyed with the soft curls on his chest, and then ran her fingers down the thin line of hair bisecting his toned belly and leading down to his manhood. She gasped as she touched it, for his erection was truly impressive. She would have drawn back then, but he grasped her hand and wrapped it around his cock as he continued teasing her nipples with an expert tongue. She felt as though she was holding an iron rod in her hand, an iron rod sheathed in the softest, finest silk. She gripped him harder, and felt him swell to even more impressive proportions between her fingers.

He tugged her tunic off, letting it fall to the floor, and then tugged off his toga and pulled her against him. She shuddered as he laid her down on the couch and she felt the full length of his unyielding body spreading over her, his rigid penis prodding against her belly as he continued stroking and caressing her with his lips and his hands. Her pussy was so hot and wet now it almost hurt, and she gasped with pleasure as he slipped two fingers inside her. He moved them gently back and forth at first, then harder and faster as she raised her hips to let them in deeper. She whimpered when he withdrew his hand, but then he thrust his knee between her thighs and his powerful torso rose above her undulating body like Neptune from the waves as he dove deep into her drenched cleft. There was a brief moment of discomfort as his large cock pushed into her, then all her resistance dissolved and she moaned in ecstasy as his rampant hardness filled her. He withdrew only to penetrate her with even more force, and she wrapped her legs around his hips and arched her back to meet each one of his thrusts. She whimpered with pleasure as he bucked and pulsed between her thighs, and the feel of his hot cum filling her was so delicious it did not matter at all that it was Helga's name on his lips as he climaxed.

Afterwards he collapsed against her, and their breaths came raggedly as they gradually recovered. She waited apprehensively for him to realise what he had done, and to take his displeasure out on her, but instead he smoothed her damp hair back from her forehead, and kissed her with the first tenderness she had experienced in a long time.

'Thank you,' he murmured drowsily. Then his head fell heavily on her breasts, and he slept peacefully for the first time since his lover's death.

Branna waited until she was sure he was sleeping soundly before gently disentangling herself, and then she slipped off the couch and back into her tunic. The lamp was out, but the first streaks of dawn were painting the sky as she tiptoed back to her room. The soft sound of footsteps at the other end of the corridor made her freeze on the threshold and strain her ears, but she heard nothing more.

It was only as she lay sleepily on her own couch, her body still tingling from Marcus Cornelius's lovemaking, that a dreadful thought brought her back to terrified wakefulness. What if there had been someone at the end of the corridor after all? And what if it had been Lavinia spying jealously on her husband and her slave? Her mouth went dry with fear. If her mistress thought she had taken Helga's place, would she meet with the same awful fate?

When Lavinia called Branna to her chamber the following morning, Branna was relieved when she treated her no differently than on any other day. There was no extra venom in her mistress's voice, or any added viciousness in the slaps and pinches she dispensed with equal fervour to all her slaves. She breathed a sigh of relief. Marcus Cornelius's nocturnal grief and consolation must have passed unnoticed.

Branna's relief was short-lived, however. The master had found both comfort and ecstasy in her arms, and was unwilling to give them up. Two nights later he found his way to her in the slave quarters, and led her to Helga's old room, where he once again drowned his sorrows in her arms and his erection in her wet and willing pussy. And as he continued to do so, she was torn between the pleasure he brought her and fear for her life. If Lavinia were to discover their secret... the thought was too terrible to ponder.

Then a dreadful possibility struck her. Perhaps the mistress already knew and was merely biding her time. Helga and her son received no warning before they were struck down. One minute they were going about their lives, and the next they were writhing in agony on their deathbeds.

Branna began taking precautions. She ate nothing that had not already been tasted by others, waiting until everyone else at the table served themselves first before helping herself to what remained, and she made sure her glass was always the last poured from the jug before she drank. The only fruit she ate was fruit she picked herself from the trees in the kitchen garden, for even Lavinia could not tamper with those.

But the strain of remaining constantly alert and defending herself began to tell. She lost weight, and jumped at the slightest sound. Exhaustion made her clumsy, and she lost count of the number of times Lavinia boxed her ears for tugging her hair when she combed it, or for being too slow to bring out her jewellery.

Even worse, her changed behaviour began to be noticed by the other slaves.

'Get this down you, girl,' Clovis commanded with brusque kindness, handing her a beaker of rich, creamy milk with a spoonful of honey stirred into it. 'You're fading away to a shadow.' He winked. 'Too many late nights with the master, eh?'

The beaker dropped from her nerveless fingers and shattered on the red tiles of the kitchen floor as she stared at Clovis in horrified despair. If he knew, then the whole household knew. And if the whole household knew, then how long before someone, eager to curry favour with the mistress, whispered the information in her ear? With haunted eyes she stared at the puddle of milk spreading across the floor, and then up at Clovis. Perhaps his offer had not been made out of kindness... perhaps he had been paid to add a little something extra to the milk...!

'By all the gods, girl, you're as nervous as a kitten!' he grumbled, and called crossly for a kitchen slave to mop up the mess. Then he picked up another beaker, poured more milk into it, added another couple of spoonfuls of honey to sweeten it, and then - much to her relief - tasted it himself. Satisfied, he handed it to her. 'And don't break this one, or I'll take it out of your wages.' He dug his elbow into her ribs. 'Take it out of your wages! Get it? Good one, huh?'

'Thank you,' she murmured, and gave him a weak smile before gratefully swallowing the milk, relishing the sweet, wholesome taste.

He examined her critically. 'That's better,' he said as she handed him back the beaker. 'You've got a bit of colour back in those cheeks of yours now.' He chuckled. 'With that white face you were starting to look like something escaped from the underworld.'

Days turned into weeks, and weeks into months, without anything untoward happening, and Branna began to relax somewhat. Clovis insisted in keeping up what he called 'his treatment' and she began to regain the weight she had lost. Perhaps Lavinia did not know, or if she did, perhaps she feared what Marcus Cornelius would do if another female member of his household conveniently ate 'something noxious'.

That day, when Lavinia called Branna to her room, she went without a flicker of suspicion. She was accustomed to her mistress's ill treatment by now. When Lavina shrieked and screamed, she simply bent her head in mock humility and let it all wash over her, secure in the knowledge that it was *her* bed the master sought when darkness fell. As for the blows, she endured them stoically. 'Yes, mistress?' she asked, forcing herself to make a brief obeisance. 'How may I serve you, mistress?'

Lavinia lolled back in her chair and an unpleasant smile curled her lips. '"How may I serve you, mistress"?' she repeated in a mockingly high-pitched voice. She took a long swallow of wine from the goblet beside her, and banged it back down on the table so hard that red droplets splattered over its smooth surface. 'You little bitch, it's not me you're serving any more, it's my husband.'

Fear tightened Branna's belly. 'I-I don't know what you mean, mistress,' she stammered defensively.

'Oh yes you do,' Lavinia hissed. 'You know exactly what I mean, you little slut.' Her head darted forward like a striking snake's. 'Do you think I'm stupid? *Do* you?'

Branna shook her head. 'No, mistress.'

'Good, because I've known about your little games for months now, but unfortunately I think my dear husband might object if another of his little playmates comes to an untimely end.' She paused thoughtfully. 'But if she were to run away instead, that would hardly be my fault, now would it?'

'B-but, I haven't run away,' Branna protested in frightened confusion.

'I know, my dear, but you're going to.' She looked over Branna's shoulder, and smiled. 'Take her away.'

Branna heard the sound of someone approaching from behind her and whirled around, but it was too late. She had a brief glimpse of what looked like a great bird swooping down, and then a sheet of heavy sackcloth descended over her, shutting out the light and trapping her beneath its weight. She screamed and kicked against it, but her cries were muffled and the more she struggled, the more entangled she became. Then she gasped as strong arms encompassed her, and she was whisked off her feet and slung over her unseen assailant's shoulder. The movement knocked the breath out of her lungs, and her mouth opened and shut soundlessly like that of a beached fish as she tried to suck air back into them.

She was carried swiftly from the room, her body jolting against her assailant's hard shoulder with every step. Sandaled feet clattered over the marble floor as she was carried out of the house, and she squealed as she was flung roughly down onto a hard surface. Then she winced as a rope was wrapped around her ankles, biting into her skin even through the thick cloth. There was a final tug as her bonds were checked, and then she was left, trussed like a chicken ready for the oven, panting and straining her ears as she tried to work out what was happening.

Her answer came when she heard the sound of hooves on a paved road, and was jolted once more. She rolled helplessly until she banged against what felt like a raised wooden partition, and realisation dawned - she was in the well of a cart!

If she had been frightened before, she was terrified now.

Where were they taking her? Lavinia had said she would be branded as a runaway, but runaways could be found, and then a chill finger touched her spine. Corpses, however, could not...

A cold perspiration broke out all over her body and she began to shiver uncontrollably. Were they taking her to some remote spot to pitch her body into the depths of the Tiber? The river surrounding the city would wipe out all memory of her brief existence as efficiently as the waters of Lethe, and her imagination painted an all too vivid picture of her impending death. The shock of the icy water, her frantic struggles as she sank beneath the cold surface wrapped in the crippling sackcloth, her lungs straining painfully as she gasped desperately for air. Some said drowning was an easy death, but she did not believe it. She shuddered and prayed her abductor would be merciful and use a knife before he threw her into a watery grave.

She held her breath and tried to slow the blood pounding through her heart and in her ears as she strained to hear a sound that would give her a clue as to where she was. To her surprise and relief, instead of dying away into the quiet of the countryside, the noise of the city seemed to be getting even louder. She could hear the rattle of hooves, the babble of the marketplace, the bellows of hucksters selling their wares, and the jolting became rougher as the cart bounced over ruts and potholes in the city's back roads. They must be leaving the main thoroughfares behind, and she winced as she was rolled from one side of the cart to the other while the constant swaying motion made her feel sick to her stomach. The air filtering through the thick cloth was hot and humid, making her feel faint and dizzy, and then a sudden realisation made her feel even weaker with dread. She recognised the smell; it was the stench of the *subura*, and terror gripped her again. Were they taking her back to Haephestus's den of depravity? Was she to suffer a living death in secret rooms deep in the city's bowels? Even drowning in the Tiber would be kinder than that!

The cart shuddered to a halt. For a few moments nothing happened, then she heard the sound of footsteps, a creaking as the back of the cart was lowered, and she was scooped up like a bundle of laundry again. The street sounds died away as she was carried into a building, and the door banged closed behind her. Her abductor carried her down a short corridor, and then flung her down onto a mercifully soft surface. She heard the sound of another door closing, and then the ominous click of a key turning in a lock. The footsteps receded into the distance, and silence descended around her.

For a long time Branna lay where she had fallen trying to regain her senses. She tested her bonds, but they were as tight as ever and she gave up trying to loosen them, sagging weakly back into the sackcloth's foreboding cocoon. The floor crackled beneath her weight, and she realised she must be lying on a straw pallet. Apart from the pain in her ankles where the ropes bit into them, she was unharmed, so far. But where was she, and what did they, whoever *they* were, intend to do with her?

A sudden furtive noise made her stiffen with dread. Someone was slowly turning the key in the lock, and apparently trying to make as little noise as possible. There was a soft clicking sound as the door opened. She closed her eyes and breathed deeply and regularly, desperately trying not to panic and pretending to be unconscious. If whomever was in the room with her believed she was helpless, she might be able to catch them off guard...

Feet padded softly towards the pallet on which she lay, and she felt someone begin fumbling with the knots at her ankles. As the ropes loosened she forced herself to remain perfectly still. Then she was rolled over and the heavy sackcloth was pulled away from her. She still could not see anything, and in the darkness of the room she felt a warm breath on her cheek as someone bent over her. She lunged upright, her fingers curling into claws as she went for her assailant's throat. He might kill her, but at least she would do him some serious damage first. Her hands fastened around his throat, and she heard a gasp of shock followed by choking sounds as she tightened her grip.

It took her a few moments to realise her assailant was not a man and, startled by this fact, she loosened her grip.

'By Toutatis,' a voice croaked and wheezed, 'I only came to say hello.'

Branna lowered her hands and peered into the darkness. '"By Toutatis"?' she repeated, unable to believe her ears. It could not be... then there was the sound of flint striking, a spark flared, and light bloomed as the wick of an oil lamp caught, whereupon Branna found herself looking at a blessedly familiar face. 'Tallis?' she gasped. 'You're alive!'

'Yes, but no thanks to you,' the other girl grumbled, gingerly rubbing her throat. 'Do you usually greet old friends by trying to throttle them to death? I must say, though, this is a nice surprise. I just wanted to see who the new girl was, and it's you.'

'And it's *you!*' Branna exclaimed with delight. But then her smile vanished as she stared more closely at her old friend, and suddenly noticed the changes in her. Tallis's wild hair had been oiled into smoothness and pulled back from her forehead, and it fell in a mass of artificial ringlets around her face. Her features were painted into a grotesque mockery of her original loveliness, her eyelids stained blue and her cheeks and lips dyed a bright red against a white cosmetic mask. Gaudy earrings jangled from her earlobes when she moved, her neck was hung with cheap bead necklaces, and when she sat down her flimsy tunic rode up to uncover her sex and the cheeks of her buttocks.

'What's happened to you?' Branna gasped. She looked around and took in her surroundings for the first time. She was in a small wooden *cubiculum* furnished with nothing but the bed she lay on, and a small table holding a jug and basin. 'And where am I?'

'What do I *look* like?' Tallis snapped, her smile bitter. Then she shrugged, and Branna realised with horror that her nipples beneath the thin material were rouged to match her lips. 'You're in a *lupanar*, my dear friend.'

Branna stared at her blankly.

'A brothel,' Tallis explained patiently. 'Remember the old bitch who bought me at the slave market? Well, that was Dolorosa, the madam of this place. Toutatis knows what her real name was before she changed it.' She laughed without humour. 'We just call her old mother misery, because it's her speciality.' The sudden sound of footsteps out in the corridor made her leap to her feet. 'By the gods, it's her. I've got to get out of here!'

But it was too late. The door swung open and the ancient harridan hobbled into the room accompanied by two hard-faced male slaves. Dolorosa immediately caught sight of Tallis cowering in a corner. 'Get out of here,' she commanded. 'You have a client waiting.' Tallis fled and the vicious hag then turned her attention to Branna. 'Get up, and take your clothes off.'

Trembling, Branna obeyed her as quickly as she could manage.

Dolorosa studied her, taking in her smooth young body. She reached for her breasts and weighed them in her gnarled fingers, and Branna winced in pain as the old woman pinched her nipples into hardness and stepped back to admire them. 'A good buy,' she said with a note of satisfaction in her harsh voice. 'The customers will pay well for this one.' She nodded towards one of the slaves, and Branna realised to her horror that he held some kind of metal implement. She cringed away in dread as he moved closer, seized her, and held her firmly against him as he brought it towards her face. She closed her eyes, and there was a grinding noise ending in a loud snap as the slave collar around her throat was wrenched off.

'There,' said mother misery, 'that takes care of that.' She smiled, revealing a row of stained and broken teeth. 'You're mine now, and don't you ever dare forget it. Cross me, and you'll regret it.' She nodded to the other male slave. 'Fetch the *aedile*,' she ordered. 'He's waiting in the anteroom.'

The young man left, and returned almost at once with a short, grey-haired man who held a scroll and a pen. He regarded Branna without interest as he wrote down her details, and then looked at Dolorosa questioningly. The old woman named a price, which was duly noted with the rest of the information.

Branna looked from mother misery to the *aedile* in horror as realisation dawned. She was now officially a whore.

CHAPTER 7

The door banged closed behind Dolorosa, leaving Branna in darkness once more, with only her miserable thoughts for company. From elsewhere in the house she could hear the low rumble of male voices, and faint shrieks of drunken laughter. It was obvious the *lupanar* was quite a lucrative business. It could not be long past midday and yet already the place was bustling like an anthill.

She stiffened as she heard the sounds of stumbling footsteps out in the corridor. There was a muttered curse, and then the thin wooden wall vibrated as a drunken body lurched against it. She sincerely hoped this was not to be her first client, but her fears were allayed by a female giggle, and then by the sound of a door opening and closing nearby. There was a brief moment of silence, followed by scuffling noises, then the giggling stopped suddenly and there was a cry of protest. Branna held her breath. The sound of a slap rang in her ears, and a shriek of pain was followed by more slurred cursing. Another slap followed the first, and then another. She tried to block out the bestial grunting and slobbering that followed, but it was impossible. She could see the scene so clearly in her mind's eye that she might as well have been in the room with the couple. She shuddered at the images in her head of a cruel hand coming down on quivering flesh, and then of a brutish mounting as the man forced himself between the thighs of the freshly spanked girl. Her own low moan of horror was lost in the louder cries penetrating the thin walls, and she put her hands over her ears to try and shut them out. That would be her own fate soon enough.

When the door opened abruptly, her first thought was that her fate had come even sooner than she expected. She looked up with frightened eyes, and then went limp with relief. 'Tallis,' she gasped. 'I thought you were...' She shuddered. 'I thought you were a client.'

'You'll get used to it,' her friend said shortly. 'In this place you either laugh or go mad, and at least old mother misery doesn't stint on the wine. Drink enough, and you won't even notice who's fucking you.'

'I don't think I could ever drink enough for that,' Branna said miserably.

'Then you won't survive,' Tallis told her bluntly. 'And some don't, believe me.' Her face clouded as she remembered and told Branna of a little dark-haired Gaul who had stabbed herself with one of her client's daggers. 'But *we* will,' she concluded firmly. 'I'm saving up to buy my freedom. Sometimes, if a customer's really pleased with you, he'll give you a little extra something for yourself. Once I get enough I'll be out of here so fast you won't see me for the dust.'

Branna smiled at her, but her heart was not in it. She had heard the same story over and over again from every other slave she had ever met, and yet for all their fine talk, they were still slaves. It seemed to her that your freedom was like your virginity - once it was gone, it was gone forever.

Her tumbling thoughts came full circle, and apprehension gripped her again. 'W-when will I have to start working?' she asked in a quavering voice. 'Tonight?'

'You haven't looked at yourself in a mirror, have you?' Tallis chuckled mirthlessly.

Branna stared at her in confusion, so Tallis left the room abruptly, and returned a moment later holding a lamp and a small mirror made of polished metal. She sat down on Branna's pallet and held the mirror up in front of her.

Branna's hand flew to her face as she stared at her reflection. Her left eyelid was purple and her lips were puffed and swollen - parting gifts from Lavinia.

'The rest of you isn't much better,' Tallis informed her grimly. 'What did they do to you, beat you before they brought you here?'

Branna looked down at her body, and for the first time noticed the marks on her skin. 'No, I must have gotten these when I was being tossed around in the back of that cart,' she said.

Tallis shrugged. 'It doesn't matter how it happened, you won't be working until they're gone.' Her mouth twisted. 'Nothing but the finest merchandise in this house; mother misery has her reputation to think of.' This time her laugh was bitter. 'If there are any marks on you the customers like to put them there themselves, and she charges them dearly for the privilege, believe me. Anyway, it'll give her time to spread the word that there's a new girl to be had,' she added shrewdly. 'After my first night I could barely walk for the next two days.'

Branna hastily pushed the thought away. She had a few days' grace, and that was all that mattered and all she cared about, for now.

Just then their little visit was interrupted when a slave boy stuck his head into the room. 'Mistress Dolorosa says you're to bring the new girl down to the *triclinium* now,' he informed Tallis.

'Dinner,' said Tallis, getting to her feet. 'And time to meet the others. Come on.'

Reluctantly, Branna stood up and followed her down the corridor, noting the number of doors they passed while averting her eyes from the obscene frescoes painted on the walls, no doubt to stimulate the customers' appetites on the way to the *cubicula*.

Downstairs, her eyes widened. Unlike her former mistress's villa, there was no atrium, just a large room full of couches and tables whose original richness had been worn away by time and frequent use. A lyre lay discarded beside a cushion in one corner.

'The reception room,' said Tallis. 'This is the dinner break, it'll be full enough again later.' She snorted. 'Dolorosa doesn't miss a trick. She makes a few extra *sesterces* selling wine to the customers while they're waiting.'

She led the way into the *triclinium* and Branna stopped on the threshold as every face turned towards her. Dolorosa sat at the head of a long table, and there must have been at least another dozen girls seated around it. A blonde girl, her body bulging with rolls of fat, sat beside a tall black girl whose ribs showed through her ebony skin; they looked like a painting of feast and famine. There were girls of all shapes and sizes and colours.

Tallis caught Branna's expression of surprise. 'Mother Dolorosa caters to all tastes,' she whispered.

The emaciated black girl reached greedily for a platter of meat, and had her hand smacked for her effort.

'Manners,' said Mother Dolorosa primly. 'Girls, meet the latest member of our little family.'

'"Little family"!' hissed Tallis beneath her breath. 'That's a good one. She'd sell her grandmother for a couple of *denarii's*.' Then in a louder voice she said, 'This is my friend, Branna,' and began introducing her to the rest of the girls.

The names went in one ear and out the other as Branna forced herself to nod and smile, but it was a relief when the girls went back to their own conversations and she could slip unobtrusively into an empty place and sit listening to their chatter. After a few moments, however, she wished she were deaf. Her appetite, already small, vanished completely as she heard the girls discussing the night's work ahead and the customers they expected to entertain. Then she discovered that the girl who normally occupied the seat in which she was sitting was indisposed after the attentions of a particularly zealous customer.

'He's a beast, that Max,' the plump little blonde declared, her body literally quivering with anger and disgust. 'Last time he had me I couldn't sit down for a week, and he nearly knocked out one of my teeth. Bastard!' she added venomously. 'I hope our lady Venus gives him some horrible disease and his cock rots off.' She bit viciously into a chunk of meat.

'Don't worry,' Tallis whispered to Branna, 'you won't get him, not yet, anyway. Old ma misery isn't that stupid. She'll start you off on the easy clients. She won't take the risk of having her new stock damaged quite so early in the game.'

This news was small consolation to Branna. The mere thought of clients made her feel sick as she made an effort to nibble at her food. The idea of attempting to escape resurfaced in her mind after all this time. It would be easier now that her iron slave collar had been removed, and the *subura* was huge. Who would notice one more small body in that seething mass of humanity? As if in answer to her unspoken thoughts, Mistress Dolorosa clapped her hands.

'No sleeping in tomorrow, girls,' she announced. 'Remember, it's bath day.'

There was a chorus of happy groans and Branna looked at her old friend enquiringly.

'Told you the old bag prided herself on running a classy house,' whispered Tallis. 'We go to the baths every two days. Actually, it's quite fun. You'll enjoy it.'

Branna smiled back, a genuine smile this time. She certainly would enjoy it. The gods had answered her prayers and given her just the opportunity she needed to get out of there, and she would grab it with both hands. There was still the evening to be got through, however, and the girls were already pushing their plates away and preparing to set about the evening's business.

'Take the new girl with you and show her a few tricks of the trade,' Dolorosa commanded, running her eyes critically over Branna. 'She's far too raw yet. She needs a bit of polish.'

Giggling, the girls led their apprehensive victim away to a communal dressing room.

'Hair first, I think,' said Nubia, the tall black girl. The others nodded in agreement, and Branna sighed with relief as she prepared to sit down in front of a mirror to have it done.

There was another chorus of giggles at her naivety. 'Not that hair, silly,' Nubia said scornfully, 'your body hair.'

'What?' Branna gasped.

'The customers like us smooth and silky,' Tallis explained. 'It won't take long.' She made Branna undress and lie down on a couch. 'Now spread your legs,' she said.

Nervously, Branna did as she was told while Nubia fetched a large jar from one of the presses. She flinched as the tall black girl began to apply the sticky unguent to her mound, and then she began to relax. It might be embarrassing, but at least it was painless. A strip of linen was then laid on top of the gum, moulded over the lips of her sex, and pressed firmly down.

'Almost finished,' Tallis crooned, and then nodded to Nubia. 'Now!' she said, and

Nubia took hold of the top edge of the cloth, and ripped it off.

Branna's mouth opened but she could not utter a sound; the pain was so monumental it took her breath away. Tears ran down her cheeks and it felt as though someone had set fire to her vulva. And to add insult to injury, the rest of the girls were laughing at her. 'You bitches!' she gasped when she could finally speak.

'Sorry,' giggled Tallis, 'but we've all been through it. Consider it an initiation.'

Nubia advanced on her with another jar and Branna flinched away, curling up to protect herself.

'It's all right,' Tallis said soothingly, 'this is to ease the pain.'

Reluctantly, Branna parted her legs again, and sighed with relief as Nubia delicately applied the cooling ointment and the sting in her labia began to ease a little.

'Armpits next,' said Tallis briskly.

It was worse now that she knew what to expect, but Nubia knew what she was doing and it was all over quickly. Her body felt strangely vulnerable now, as if she was more than naked, and she quickly slipped her tunic back on to hide herself.

'You hair now,' Tallis announced.

Branna glared at her. 'What hair,' she demanded crossly. 'I've got none left!'

'What do you call this then?' Tallis tugged a stray strand, inspecting Branna's head critically. 'It may be fair already, but it's not quite the shade our clients admire. We'll need to dye it.'

By the time they had finished with her, Branna did not recognise the reflection staring back from the mirror. Her hair was now a brassy blonde, her eyebrows had been plucked within an inch of their lives, and her features were a cosmetic mask, her eyes darkened with kohl and blue paste, her lips and cheeks brightly rouged. The girls rallied round her to loan her various bits of jewellery, and her newly acquired bracelets, earrings and bangles jangled irritatingly with her slightest movement.

'There, what do you think?' asked Tallis, hovering over her expectantly.

'I think my face will crack in two if I smile,' Branna muttered. 'No wonder Lavinia was so bad-tempered, having to go through this every day.'

'It'll be all worth it when you get those extra tips from your clients,' Tallis assured her, just as the little slave boy burst into the dressing room.

'Hurry up,' he panted. 'Mistress Dolorosa is furious. There's someone waiting for you, Tallis!'

She gasped and her hand flew to her mouth. 'By the gods, my client! I forgot all about him. Young Cassus the scribe said he'd come early tonight.'

'Scribe?' asked Branna, grabbing Tallis's arm as she made to run for the door. 'Does that mean he writes letters for people?'

Tallis nodded. 'Yes he does... so?'

'Do you think he'd write one for me?'

'If I asked him to he would,' Tallis confirmed. 'He's a lovely boy, and besotted with me. But who would you want to write a letter to?'

Branna looked around her furtively before whispering something in her friend's ear. Tallis smiled conspiratorially. 'Ah, I see. Of course he'll do it. I'll make sure of it.'

When the other girls also left to go about their duties, Branna was smiling, too. It was not a pleasant smile as she turned her head this way and that, however, contemplating her face in the mirror. The cosmetics did not quite hide the fact that her eye was still puffy, and her body ached everywhere, but this was a blessing in disguise if it put off the time until when she would have to start working. And if her plan did not fail, she might escape that evil fate entirely. Then the door opened again and her smile vanished at the sight of Dolorosa, whose own face was creased in a scowl.

'What do you think you're doing lounging around in here like a lady?' the old woman demanded. 'I didn't pay good money for you so you could just sit on your arse. On your feet, there's work to be done!'

Branna's mouth went dry. 'B-but, I thought I was not to begin until my eye had healed and—'

'You're not,' Dolorosa snapped, 'but we're busy, and you can still fetch and carry, can't you? Anyway, who's going to notice your marks if you keep your clothes on?' She looked at Branna's grubby tunic. 'Get yourself out of that rag and into something presentable, then get your arse downstairs.' Turning on her heels, she bustled out of the dressing room.

The press in the corner of the room held several gaudy tunics made of flimsy silk. Branna went through them, frantically trying to find the least revealing one, but it was a hopeless task. Even the tunic she eventually picked was obscenely short, barely skimming over the curves of her buttocks, and the thin blue silk revealed rather than concealed her smooth body beneath it. No matter how hard she tried to hitch up the top, the garment was cut so cunningly that it slid down to reveal the upper half of her nipples.

She looked at herself in the mirror again, and groaned. She could *not* go downstairs looking like that...

A sudden sharp smack made the cheeks of her exposed bottom quiver and redden. She squealed with shock and pain and whirled around. Dolorosa had returned, and she was not pleased. 'I told you to get your lazy arse downstairs, you little slut, and here you are still parading in front of the mirror admiring yourself!' she spat vehemently. 'Now shift yourself before you feel my hand again!' Then gripping Branna by the wrist, she dragged her through the door and all the way to the *culina*, where she seized a jar of wine and thrust it into her hands.

'Go and serve the clients,' she ordered. 'And make sure they pay you, and always remember to smile. They come here to escape their bad-tempered wives, not to look at another miserable face.'

Clutching the wine jug like a shield before her, Branna walked towards the reception area. On the threshold she paused and swallowed as she was met by a gust of hot air. The room had been empty before, but now every table was crowded, and the lyre player was attempting to make herself heard above the din of men laughing and playing dice as girls giggled and flaunted themselves in an attempt to attract their attention.

Nubia was sitting on the lap of a fat old man, stroking his face as his hand fumbled beneath the hem of her brief tunic. The plump blonde girl was perched on the edge of a table, leaning forward while two men grappled with her enormous breasts, and she laughed as they each sucked on her rouged nipples. Then she pulled herself away, murmured something to them, and rising led them both towards the stairs.

If Branna had hoped to remain unnoticed, she was disappointed. There was a momentary lull in the rowdy atmosphere when she appeared, and then a chorus of raucous cheers greeted her entry.

'Over here, sweetheart!'

'No, over here, honey!'

Smiling men kept beckoning her towards their tables with obscene noises and gestures, so gritting her teeth, she plastered a smile on her face and made her way through the hot and crowded room.

The ensuing evening was an exercise in humiliation. As she bent over to pour the wine, her breasts spilled out and her skimpy tunic rode up her hips. Greedy hands groped at her breasts, pinching her nipples so hard she winced with pain as more enquiring fingers crawled up between her thighs and attempted to pry their way into her pussy.

At one point, fumbling with the wine jug and the fistful of coins she had received as payment, she stumbled and dropped them all. They scattered across the floor, and as she knelt to collect them someone planted a foot on her bare bottom and sent her sprawling facedown across the floor, much to the amusement of those all around her.

Then at long last, in the small hours of the morning, the nightmare ended. The last drunk was escorted from the premises, and the yawning girls made their way to their beds, this time to sleep.

Wearily, Branna handed over the money she had collected to Dolorosa, who counted it carefully before smiling at her. 'A good start,' the old crone said approvingly. 'There is a third more here than usual. You have done well.' Her lips parted in a broken-toothed smile. 'And if you can make this much just selling wine, just think how much more you'll make for me selling your body.'

Branna shuddered and her mouth set in a grim line as she made her way back up the stairs to the little room that was now hers. If all went well, by the same time tomorrow she would be long gone. She simply *had* to get away, and she could only pray the gods were on her side.

'Wake up, sleepyhead!' a bright voice insisted, rousing Branna. Tallis was perched on the edge of her pallet, smiling down at her almost happily.

Branna sat up slowly, glaring at the other girl. Her head ached and her mouth tasted terrible. 'I don't know what you're looking so cheerful about,' she grumbled. 'I feel as if I've just been run over by a chariot.'

'You'll soon get used to it,' Tallis informed her callously, and winked. 'Anyway, I'm entitled to be cheerful. I made a few extra *sesterces* last night, and we're going to the baths this morning. Remember?'

'Yes, of course,' Branna said, brightening. She swung her legs out of bed eagerly, but then her face fell. 'I haven't got anything to wear, though,' she grumbled. 'I can't possibly go out in that... that thing I had on last night.'

'No need to,' Tallis said. 'Your own tunic's been washed and mended. See?' She shook it out and held it up.

Branna sighed with relief. It might be worn and patched, but at least it was decent. She tugged it on over her nakedness, and they hurried to breakfast together.

The other girls were already there, in various stages of wakefulness, some yawning and resentful at being dragged from their beds so early, others bright-eyed and looking forward to a break from their routine and a relaxing morning at the baths.

As she reached for a slice of bread slathered with honey, Branna asked casually, 'So, do we just walk down to the baths by ourselves?'

Everyone looked at her incredulously for an instant, and then burst out laughing.

'Are you mad?!' Nubia exclaimed. 'Old ma misery wouldn't trust us as far as she could throw us.'

'Not since that little Gaul tried to run off and chuck herself in the Tiber,' chimed in the plump blonde, whose name was Bellinda. 'Ever since then we're better guarded than the Vestal Virgins themselves!'

'A bit late in the day for that, in your case,' sniggered her neighbour, who instantly received a dig in the ribs.

'She's got those big bruisers of hers watching our every move,' Bellinda then went on. 'Just in case a girl shows a bit of free enterprise.'

'You're just annoyed because they stopped you going into that back alley with a pretty Phoenician sailor the other day,' mocked another girl.

'So, what's wrong with earning a bit on the side?' Bellinda asked. 'The old bitch makes enough off us already. Zeus knows she wouldn't miss it.'

Branna's heart sank as her hope of an easy escape vanished. While the girls continued to squabble amiably, she wracked her brains for a way around the situation, and began to smile to herself as an idea dawned. Now, if only Tallis would agree to it...

'You want me to start an argument?' Tallis qualified. They were safely back in Branna's room. 'Well, that won't be hard. But are you sure you know what you're doing? I can give you a few *sesterces*, but that won't last long. How are you going to survive when that's gone? Where are you going to hide? Ma Dolorosa doesn't take too kindly to being thwarted, to put it mildly. She'll have her slaves hunting high and low for you in no time. And what about Marcus Cornelius, your previous owner? From what you've said he thinks you've run away. It's far too dangerous.'

'And staying here isn't?' Branna demanded bitterly. 'That old sow wouldn't care if her clients murdered the lot of us, provided they paid her enough for the privilege. You know as well as I do that she could go down to the slave market and replace us all tomorrow.' She shook her head. 'But if you don't want to help me...' her voice trailed off and she looked hopefully at Tallis.

'Oh, all right, but don't say I didn't warn you,' Tallis relented. 'And if they catch you, there's nothing more I can do to help.'

'I'll take that risk.' Branna beamed at her, and then hugged her warmly. 'Thank you!'

'You won't be saying that if it all goes wrong,' Tallis warned. 'But I'll do my best.'

When the girls eventually set off for the baths, Tallis's few precious *sesterces* were concealed in a small bag tied around Branna's neck on a leather thong and tucked down between her breasts. They would be enough to buy her bread and a few nights' lodging somewhere.

It was a strange sensation walking towards the baths. They marched two-by-two, escorted by four of Dolorosa's biggest male slaves, and with her leading the way, they seemed more like a family of well-bred daughters with their grandmother than the denizens of a notorious whorehouse. Or at least they would have had the girls not been eyed up lecherously by every man they passed along the way. It dawned on Branna that this was not so much an exercise in cleanliness as a regular advertising campaign.

By the time they reached their destination they were perspiring and covered in dust, and as they entered the baths a sweet coolness washed over them, the sound of water lapping against marble a soothing balm to the ears after the noise and commotion of the streets.

'Right girls,' said Dolorosa briskly, 'clothes and jewellery off.'

Branna clutched the thong around her neck in a panic. She could not leave her money. What if it was stolen? Taking advantage of the fact that all the girls were milling about she ducked into an alcove, lifted the little leather bag from the thong round her neck, parted her legs, and very carefully slipped it up as far inside her vagina as she could. Her few precious sesterces would be safe enough, for now.

As she rejoined the others the coins moved gently in their bag with every step she took, and sent strangely pleasurable sensations through her. She shivered as she undressed, her nipples hardening in response to the subtly delicious thrills coursing through her pelvis with her every movement.

'Are you all right?' Tallis asked her anxiously. 'You've gone awfully red.'

'Yes, I'm fine,' Branna replied, controlling her breathing with difficulty. She turned away to hand her bundle of clothing to an attendant, her face flushed.

Without their clothes the girls were a motley group. Bellinda's rolls of white flesh quivered gently as she walked, her huge breasts bouncing with her every step, while Nubia's tall black body looked more skeletal than ever. Looking at them, Branna was amazed by the variety of men's hunger, and her lips twisted in distaste. No doubt even Dolorosa's ancient shrivelled body with its sagging teats had its perverse admirers, and she wondered if it was still on the market.

There was no sitting around laughing and chatting at the baths. Time meant money in Dolorosa's book. The girls were quickly oiled and scraped with a *strigil*, and then they all made their way through to the *caldarium*.

'Are you sure you're all right, Branna?' Tallis persisted in asking her as they walked along the corridor. 'You've gone absolutely scarlet. Is the heat too much for you?'

The heat was not too much, but the pouch of coins tucked inside her pussy was; it was driving her mad with excitement. Her every movement set off sensations that threatened to make her lose control of herself. Her fingers itched to slide down her belly to the moist lips of her sex and bring relief from the tantalising pleasure coursing through her. 'I told you, I'm fine,' she replied again breathlessly.

Thankfully, before Tallis could enquire any further, they entered the *caldarium* and billowing clouds of steam enveloped them, hiding Branna's blushing cheeks. Carefully she walked down the steps, and as she slid beneath the surface of the scalding water, her inadvertent gasps mingled with those of the other girls.

Closing her eyes she leaned back and allowed the hot water to lap against her skin as she tried to control the ecstasy mounting inside her - but it was impossible. The gentle currents of the bath merely aggravated how sensitive her pussy had become, and unable to bear it any longer, she looked around her furtively. It was hard to see through the steam and no one was paying any attention to her, so with a sigh of relief she slid her hand between her thighs and, careful not to attract attention, began to stroke herself, parting the lips of her sex and sucking in her breath as the hot water gently seeped inside. Shuddering slightly she slipped first one finger, and then another one, inside her cleft and began to move them in and out rhythmically, slowly at first and then faster and faster as her pleasure mounted and she pushed the bag of coins deeper and deeper inside her. Biting her lip to hold back the moans of ecstasy threatening to escape, she gave herself up to an explosive climax that made her whole body tremble. Her back arched, she gave a muffled groan, and she sagged back against the wall of the pool.

Tallis looked at her with concern. 'Let's get out of here and into the *frigidarium*,' she said. 'This water's obviously too hot for you.'

'Yes, all right...' Branna agreed.

In the *frigidarium*, Branna gasped with shock as the icy water hit her body. It woke her up completely, and suddenly she had never felt so full of energy. As she got dressed again optimism filled her. She retrieved the tiny bag of money, which was soaking wet now from its sojourn in her pussy, and hung it around her neck again. Her plan was bound to work. In another hour she would be free at last. She could hardly bear the waiting as the other girls finished their ablutions. They seemed to take forever, getting dressed with maddening slowness whilst laughing and chattering and fixing each other's hair. But at long last they were finished with their primping, and lined up for the long trek back to the brothel.

As the procession wound its way through the city, Branna's stomach churned with anticipation and anxiety. She kept wondering when Tallis would make her move, and in her impatience it began to seem as if the other girl had forgotten all about her promise.

Then, at last, Tallis suddenly shrieked, 'You fat cow! Watch what you're doing!' She shoved Bellinda away from her. 'You almost had me in the gutter!'

'Wha - what are you talking about?!' Bellinda exclaimed, clearly mystified by the sudden outburst. 'I never even touched you!'

'Considering the size of your backside, it's no wonder you didn't notice,' Tallis said rudely, pushing the other girl away from her again with such force that Bellinda stumbled and nearly fell. '*Bellinda*, my arse,' Tallis mocked scornfully. 'They should have named you Balaena, the fucking whale. Zeus knows you've got enough blubber on you.'

Bellinda squealed in outrage at the insult. 'Shut your mouth, you scrawny little shit,' she yelled. 'At least my customers know they're getting a *real* woman, not some skinny titless freak!'

With a shriek of anger Tallis flung herself on the other girl, scratching and clawing at her like an enraged cat. In a moment the two girls were rolling together on the ground, spitting and screaming, while Dolorosa stood by yelling at them both to stop at once. Eager for any entertainment to brighten the day, a laughing, jeering crowd of men began gathering around them, adding to the general mayhem.

With a grunt of annoyance the slave who had been marching alongside Branna stalked to the front of the line, leaving her unguarded as he unwisely went to try and pull the fighting girls apart. So, taking a deep breath and summoning her courage, Branna took one step backwards, and then another, and then another. She looked around her furtively, but no one had noticed; everyone's attention was fixed on the catfight as people nudged each other and took bets as to which girl would emerge victorious. Taking her courage in hand she turned and slipped into the nearest alleyway, where she promptly took to her heels, running as fast as she could deeper and deeper into the slums of the *subura*.

By the time the stitch in her side forced her to stop and catch her breath, the noise of the catfight was nothing but a distant memory. Panting, she doubled over to ease the pain in her side. When it had dissipated she straightened up and looked around her. She had absolutely no idea where she was.

She was standing in a small square bounded on all sides by decrepit tenements. Ragged children played in the dust as their weary mothers fought a losing battle against dirt and flies. A shabby stallholder had set up in one corner of the square and was attempting to sell strips of cooked meat, while across from him a dingy tavern appeared to be doing a desultory trade in cheap wine. She received a few curious glances, but nothing more than that. This was obviously a place where people minded their business and let others get on with their own.

The smell of the meat was hardly appetising, nevertheless Branna's stomach growled in response. She had to eat something to keep up her strength, and she reached for the small bag around her neck anxiously, afraid she might have lost it in her headlong flight. She breathed a sigh of relief when she felt it still there, heavy with a handful of Tallis's hard earned *sesterces*. Trying to look as casual as possible, she sauntered across to the food stall.

'I'll have that piece there,' she said to the vendor, pointing at the least burnt slice. 'How much is it?'

The stallholder named his price, and Branna realised she had a new problem. She knew the names of the various coins, and had watched while Fabius paid with them at the market, but this was the first time she had actually possessed any of her own. She picked out the two smallest coins from her meagre store, and handed them over.

'Thanks,' the man said, winking at her, and she could tell from his sly smirk that she had seriously overpaid him.

Cursing herself for her stupidity, she walked away from him chewing ravenously on the stringy meat. Once she had forced down the last mouthful she wiped her greasy hands over her hair, trying to tone down the brassy blonde dye, and then tore a thin strip of cloth from the bottom of her tunic and pulled her hair back away from her face. Perhaps now she would be less noticeable while she looked for a place to stay where she could decide what to do next.

Smoothing down her tunic, she walked across the square and into the tavern, ignoring the lewd comments of the men seated at the tables.

The tavern keeper looked up from wiping a beaker on his grubby apron. 'Yes?' he asked in surprise. 'What can I do for you?'

'I want a room,' Branna stated bluntly.

He looked at her as though she was mad, and then laughed. 'A room, sweetheart? What do you think this is, Nero's fucking palace? I've got no place to put you.' He winked at her. 'Unless you fancy sharing a bed with me and the wife.'

Disgust gripped her. 'I've got money,' she said hastily and hopefully. 'I can pay my way.'

He stared at her thoughtfully for moment, and greed won. 'Well, I suppose I could put a pallet down in the storeroom,' he muttered. 'Nothing fancy, mind, but at least it'd be a roof over your head for the night.'

'I'll take it,' Branna said eagerly.

His eyes narrowed. 'Let's see your money first, though.'

She rummaged in the little leather bag, produced a small silver coin, and held it up. 'How long can I stay for this?'

'Three days,' he said at once, looking at her shrewdly as he noted how hungrily the men in the tavern were eying her nubile young body. 'Or five days if you lend a hand serving the customers. I'll even throw in one meal a day,' he added generously.

'Fine,' she agreed, and handed over the coin.

The man bit it and grinned at her, revealing a row of broken teeth. 'Done,' he said, spat in his hand, and held it out to her.

She shook it reluctantly, and then wiped her palm surreptitiously on her tunic.

'Follow me, young woman.' He called for his son to look after the place in his absence and led her through a small door at the back of the tavern into the storeroom.

Amphorae were stacked up against the walls and there was barely space enough to turn around. The room smelled of sour wine, and she could hear the telltale scuffling of rats in the walls. The floor was nothing but tramped-down earth, and she sensed its dampness through the thin soles of her sandals, but it was better than nothing, and she would be sleeping there as a free woman. Her spirits rose. It was the first step, no matter how small. She had a place to stay, and work, too. Perhaps if she did well, they might come to some agreement. It would give her a breathing space before she made her next move. But it was better not to show too much enthusiasm, or her new landlord and employer might raise the price of his rent. 'I suppose it will have to do,' she said ungraciously.

'Good, now let's find you an apron and get you started.'

Chapter 8

The next few days were hard work, but satisfying. Branna learned to serve wine while avoiding the advances of her customers, always softening the blow of her rejection with a smile and a joke. At the end of each day her feet ached, her hair smelled of sour grapes and lamp smoke, and she sank gratefully onto her thin pallet, but at least it was 'clean' work. Lentus, the tavern-keeper, seemed pleased with her efforts, and she had even made a few tips to add to her meagre store of coins. She began to relax. It seemed she had done it - she had, at long last, escaped from slavery.

On her fourth day in the tavern, she was serving customers as usual when the door opened and she turned towards the newcomer with a welcoming smile.

'What can I get you, sir?' she asked, and then she dropped the amphora she was holding. It shattered into hundreds of pieces, spilling wine everywhere. She stared at the new customer in horror, and then turned around with the intention of running, but a hand gripped her hair and hauled her back.

'Thought you'd got away with it, didn't you?' growled Catus, Dolorosa's head slave. He tugged viciously on her hair, bringing tears of pain to her eyes. 'Earned me a beating you did, you cunning little bitch. But you'll get yours. Old ma misery doesn't take kindly to runaways. I wouldn't like to be in your sandals when she gets her hands on you.' He reached into the breast of his tunic, pulled out a small bag, and flung it towards Lentus. 'There you go, mate. Thanks for looking after her for us.'

Branna looked at Lentus in horror. 'You betrayed me!' she gasped.

Lentus shrugged. 'Sorry, love,' he said, weighing the bag of coins in his hand. 'But business is business. I've got a wife and a family to support, and Dolorosa's a bad enemy to make.' He was still counting the coins as Catus bound her hands and dragged her out of the tavern.

Branna stumbled after him with despair settling over her heart like a black cloud blotting out the sun. There was no hope. She would be a slave until she died.

'You little trollop!' Dolorosa slapped Branna's face so hard the girl's ears rang. 'How dare you make a fool of me like that?' Then the old woman's mood changed and she wrung her hands as her face creased into wrinkles of self-pity. 'I put a roof over your head and food in your mouth and this is how you repay me?'

Branna stared at the evil old harridan in total disbelief. Was that how the loathsome hag saw herself, as some kind of good-hearted benefactress? The woman was a procuress. She made her living selling the bodies of unfortunate girls who had the ill luck to fall into her greedy, grasping hands. Rage overwhelmed her and she spat on the floor at Dolorosa's feet. 'Hypocrite!' she cried. 'In that case you should be grateful to me for running away. That makes one less mouth for you to feed out of the kindness of your rotten heart. Oh!' she gasped as Dolorosa's wizened hand lashed out again, and cradling her throbbing cheek she gave the woman a bitter smile. 'Be careful,' she advised, 'better not damage the merchandise. You might have to lower the price.'

Now it was Dolorosa's turn to smile, and it was not a pleasant sight. 'Don't you worry your pretty little head about that, my dear. I have a very special customer in mind for you. By the time he's finished with you, you'll be marked from arse to elbow and won't be running anywhere for a long time.' Her evil smile widened. 'In fact, you'll be hard put to sit down for a week.'

'W-what do you mean?' Branna's courage abruptly deserted her.

'Oh, you'll find out soon enough,' Dolorosa promised ominously. 'And we'll see how cocky you are then, my fine lady.' She nodded at Catus, who had been standing smirking in the background. 'Take her to her room, and this time make sure she stays there, otherwise you'll be sorry. Just you remember there are men out there who'd pay good money to break in a pretty young fellow like you. I don't normally cater to those kinds of perverts, but one more mistake and I'll make an exception with you.'

Catus's smirk disappeared and the colour drained from his face. 'Yes, mistress, of course, mistress, anything you say, mistress,' he grovelled. 'She won't get away this time, I swear it by all the gods.'

'Good,' Dolorosa snapped, 'then we understand each other.' She waved a shrivelled hand dismissively. 'Then go and do as you're told, and properly this time.'

Nodding obsequiously, Catus gripped Branna's arm and hauled her roughly from the room.

'Let go of me!' she protested, trying to wrench herself free as he dug his fingers viciously into her wrist. 'You're hurting me!'

'I'll hurt you even more if you don't shut up and behave yourself,' he snarled, dragging her along beside him. 'I've already had a beating, and if you think I'm letting some stinking catamite stick his cock up my backside because of you, then you've got another thing coming.'

He pushed open the door of her old room, shoved her down across the pallet, and leaned over her, grabbing both her nipples and twisting them between his thumb and forefinger until she whimpered. 'But you'll get what's coming to you, bitch,' he promised quietly, his garlic-laden breath foul in her face. Then he flung her away from him and strode towards the door.

On the threshold he paused, and grinned back at her tauntingly. 'And when he's reaming the arse off you, you can think of me.' The door banged shut and she was left alone in the dim lamplight.

She sat up, rubbing her aching nipples. Fear lay like a heavy stone in her belly and a wave of depression engulfed her. To enjoy a brief taste of freedom, and then have it snatched away again suddenly, was worse than never having been free at all. She might have shared the storeroom of the wine shop with the rats, but at least the small space, and her body, had been hers. A sob caught in her throat. She was never going to get away, not ever. Not until she was old and raddled and flung out to beg, or to sell her sagging body on the dockside, would she be free. Bending over and clutching her belly, which hurt from the depth of her despair, she bit her fists and wept.

But then a furtive noise snapped her out of her self-pity, and she realised the door was creaking open again. Wondering if her punishment was to begin already, she sat up and braced herself for the worst.

'Are you all right?' Tallis slipped into the room and closed the door quietly behind her. She stared at her friend's tearstained face in dismay. 'Did she have you beaten?'

Branna laughed bitterly. 'Beaten? Oh no, combining business with pleasure is much more profitable. She's got a special customer in mind for me.'

'Oh no,' Tallis gasped, 'not—' she bit off whatever name she had been about to speak and forced an unconvincing smile. 'Don't worry about it. I'm sure she's exaggerating. You'll be fine,' she went on doggedly, but the expression on her face belied her reassuring words.

Realisation dawned on Branna, and made her feel even sicker to her stomach. 'It's that Max fellow Bellinda was talking about, isn't it, the one who hurt her so badly she was laid-up for a week, the one all the other girls are terrified of, too?' She grabbed Tallis's wrist urgently. 'It is him, isn't it?'

'I don't know,' Tallis said with little conviction. 'She was probably only trying to scare you.' But her face had gone white and her eyes would not quite meet Branna's. 'But even if it is him,' she went on quickly, 'it might not be so bad, not if he's in a good mood and you do exactly what he tells you to.'

'Oh, wonderful,' Branna said sarcastically. 'If I give in to whatever perversions he has in mind, I might, I just *might*, be allowed to come out of it in one piece. No wonder that old sow was so pleased with herself,' she went on bitterly. 'She gets her revenge, and a fat purse into the bargain.'

Tallis glanced nervously at the door, as if expecting Dolorosa to walk in at any moment. 'Keep your voice down,' she whispered urgently. 'You never know who might be out there listening.'

'So what? What else can she do to me?'

'Kill you and have your body dumped in a sack in the Tiber,' Tallis informed her bluntly. 'It's happened before when a customer's taken things a little too far. Who cares if there's one whore more or less in the world? There's always plenty more where we came from.'

'I'm not frightened of dying,' Branna said quietly. 'Better to be with Cerdoc than to live like this.' Yet as soon as the words were out of her mouth, she realised they were false. Death itself truly did not scare her. That was true enough. It was the thought of leaving this world with her accounts unsettled that made her balk. She owed a debt of blood for Cerdoc, and for everything that had happened to her since then. Her mouth set grimly. She was Iceni, and the Iceni paid their debts in full, with interest.

'Are you all right?' Tallis asked her anxiously. 'For a moment there you looked quite strange.'

'I'm fine,' Branna assured her, forcing a brave smile. 'I'm just really hungry. Do you think old ma misery is going to let me eat, or am I to sit here and contemplate my sins and my upcoming punishment on an empty stomach?'

'That's why I was sent up, to fetch you down to dinner. She says you're not to be let out of your room alone, just in case.'

'Just in case *what?*' Branna laughed bitterly. 'Just in case I fall on my sword and deprive her of the pleasure of seeing me punished? Just in case I seduce Catus into letting me run away again?' She spread her hands. 'See, no sword, and I wouldn't touch that whining bastard, Catus, with a twenty-foot oar.' She stood up and linked arms with her friend. 'Come on, let's go and show that old bitch what stern stuff we're made of.'

At dinner, Branna forced herself to act as if she did not have a care in the world. She ate and drank heartily, told jokes she had heard at the tavern, chatted gaily with the rest of the girls, and every now and then even forced herself to smile at Catus and Dolorosa.

The old woman smiled back, and licked her lips like a cat with a particularly juicy mouse at its mercy. 'I'm glad to see you in such good spirits, my dear,' she wheezed. 'The customers like to see a happy face.' Her eyes narrowed with malicious amusement. 'And I have one who is eager to meet you, very eager, indeed. In fact, he can hardly wait to get his hands on you.' She paused for effect. 'Therefore, I told him he could have the pleasure of your company this very night.'

The colour drained from Branna's face and she laid down her spoon, the food she had eaten suddenly a lead weight in her stomach. 'T-tonight?' she managed, her mouth dry.

'This very night,' Dolorosa repeated with relish. She sipped her wine and smiled at Branna again almost sweetly. 'Oh dear,' she said with mock sympathy, 'lost that pretty smile, have we? What a pity. I'm afraid you'll have to find it again. I wouldn't advise you to make him feel unwelcome. He might get upset, and who knows what he might do then.'

'You vindictive old bitch,' Branna hissed. 'I hope you die writhing in agony and your spirit wanders lost and wailing for all eternity.'

The rest of the girls fell silent, holding their breath as they waited for Dolorosa's reaction to this sinister curse.

'Hush, my dear,' the old woman said placidly, but her smile looked fixed, 'that's no way to talk to your elders.' She shook her head sadly. 'But never mind, I'm sure tonight's little lesson will teach you a few good manners.' She put down her beaker to indicate the meal was over, and her smile abruptly disappeared as she looked around the table at the apprehensive girls. 'Now take her away and prepare her,' she commanded.

As the girls washed and dressed her hair and applied the requisite thick layer of cosmetics to her already lovely face, Branna was reminded of the last time she had sat in front of the mirror, with one significant difference. This time there was none of the laughing and joking and giggling that had accompanied her first experience in the dressing room. Instead, the girls worked in deadly silence, as if they were preparing a young and beautiful corpse for its untimely grave. 'I wish you would all say something,' she declared finally. 'I'm not dead *yet*.'

'You'll wish you were before the night is out,' Bellinda muttered, and received an elbow in the ribs for her trouble. 'Ouch!' she protested, glaring at Nubia accusingly. 'What was *that* for?'

'Shut up,' Nubia muttered. 'Talk like that is not going to help her any.' She smiled nervously at Branna. 'You'll be fine,' she reassured her. 'By this time tomorrow you'll be wondering what all the fuss was about.'

'Lying isn't going to help either,' Bellinda snapped. She glanced furtively towards the door, and lowered her voice. 'I still have some of the poppy juice old ma misery gave me to kill the pain after the last time the bastard had me. If I gave you a dose now, you wouldn't know what was happening. He could do whatever he wanted to you, and you would hardly notice.'

The thought was very tempting, and for a moment Branna seriously considered it, but then she shook her head. 'No thanks,' she said regretfully. 'I appreciate your kindness, but I think I had better have my wits about me.'

'It's up to you,' Bellinda conceded. 'But if I'd known what he was like, I would have taken the poppy juice.' She shuddered at the memory of the pain and humiliation she had suffered at this dreaded customer's hands. 'I still get bad dreams in which the bastard's coming after me again. Still, not to worry, because here I am, alive and well, and telling the tale.' She patted Branna's cheek. 'And you will be too, love, just grit your teeth and bear it. It won't last forever.' Her hand flew to her mouth. 'Oh, I almost forgot to warn you. For the sake of all the gods, whatever you do, don't mention his little... er, you know, problem.'

'What problem?' Branna asked blankly.

Bellinda avoided her eyes, looking as if she regretted opening her mouth. 'I can't tell you,' she muttered. 'He swore that if I ever told anyone he would come back and kill me.' She bit her lip anxiously. 'You'll find out soon enough,' she stated, and refused to say another word.

All too soon Branna was ready, her hair curled, her lips and cheeks stained red, her body washed and perfumed. The flimsy tunic was slipped up over her body, and she stared in dismay at her half naked reflection in the mirror. Her kohl-rimmed eyes looked back at her from the polished metal, all the cosmetics in the world unable to conceal the fear in their depths.

'About time, too,' Dolorosa snapped, bustling impatiently into the room. She clapped her hands imperiously. 'Hurry up, girls, get downstairs at once. We don't want to keep our clients waiting.' Branna began to follow the other girls out, but the old woman caught her by the tunic and held her back. 'Not you, nothing but the best for Max, so you've got the finest room in the house.'

'Is... is...' Branna's mouth was so dry with anxiety she could barely speak. She swallowed, and tried again. 'Is he here?' she asked, her voice weak with fear.

'Can hardly wait to meet him, can you, my lovely little slut?' Dolorosa mocked. 'Well, he'll be here soon enough. You'll just have to be patient.' She started for the door, but Branna remained exactly where she was, rooted to the spot with terror. 'Come along, girl, move yourself. Or do I have to get Catus to carry you?'

Branna forced her leaden limbs to obey and followed the old hag out of the room and along the corridor, at the end of which Dolorosa produced a large key from the folds of her tunic, unlocked the door, and threw it open with a flourish.

Even in her apprehensive state, Branna was impressed. The room was a far cry from her bare little *cubiculum*. It was large, light and airy, and it was obvious no expense had been spared in its decoration. Three of the walls were draped with silk hangings half-concealing the colourful frescoes beneath them, while the fourth wall was almost entirely hidden beneath a huge mirror that must have cost a small fortune to make. The couch was carved and gilded, and at its foot rested a large cedar chest. A small matching table stood beside the bed holding a pitcher of wine, two glasses and several small bowls filled with olives, fresh fruit and sweetmeats. A charcoal brazier in one corner, a handful of herbs smouldering inside it, provided a gentle perfumed heat against the chill of the evening, and two oil lamps hung from chains in the ceiling that gave out a soft, sensual light.

The effect should have been one of warmth and comfort, but somehow it was not. Despite the brazier, Branna shivered as she stood on the threshold. She felt misery and oppression in the air of the room, as if dark memories still lingered in the folds of the silk hangings. She looked at them more closely, and made out faint sinister brown stains on the luxurious material, stains no amount of careful laundering had been able to remove, and suddenly the warm scented air seemed to quiver with the silent echoes of screams. Goose pimples broke out on her skin. Whatever had happened in this room in the past had left its mark on the present. Then a sharp shove between her shoulder blades sent her stumbling into it, and the door was banged closed behind her. The key turned in the lock and she was left with nothing but her own thoughts and whatever evil forces haunted the room for company while she waited for her dreaded customer.

She walked over to the couch and sat down, but then what sounded like a soft sigh stirred the hangings directly behind her and she leapt to her feet again, looking around frantically. There was no rational explanation for the sound; she was completely alone. A superstitious fear made her shiver, and she wondered if this was where the little Gaul had killed herself, and if her restless spirit still walked.

A movement glimpsed in the corner of her eye made her turn quickly towards it, and then she giggled nervously as she encountered nothing but her own reflection in the large mirror.

To distract herself from her fears she ventured towards the head of the bed, lifted the hanging to examine the frescoes beneath it, and gasped with shock. They appeared to have been painted by the same artist who had decorated the rest of the establishment, but these frescoes made the ones out in the corridors and in the reception area look like children's drawings. Here was depicted Pasiphae, wife of King Minos of Crete, as she gave herself to the bull that fathered the Minotaur upon her. Her mouth was stretched wide in a cry of mingled agony and ecstasy as she was pierced by the beast's huge phallus, and Branna quickly let the hanging swing back to cover the bestial scene. Then she poured herself a glass of wine and drank it down quickly.

Fortified by the alcohol, she continued exploring the luxurious room. The cedar chest at the foot of the couch caught her eye, and she looked at it in bewilderment, unable to understand why a clothes chest was needed in a room used only for temporary assignations. Wondering what was in it, curiosity overcame her trepidation and she lifted the lid.

This time her gasp was even louder as she stared at the contents of the chest. There were several whips, something that looked like a child's bat covered in leather, an enormous penis carved out of wood, a short length of chain with what looked like some kind of clip dangling from each end, and something that looked like a piece from a horse's harness.

The sound of footsteps out in the corridor made her drop the lid of the chest and whirl around to face the door, her heart pounding as the key turned in the lock and the door swung open. She stared at the man swaying on the threshold, her eyes widening in disbelief. 'You!' she gasped.

He was not wearing his uniform, and the only weapon he carried was a dagger tucked into his belt, but she would have recognised him anywhere. His grinning face was branded forever on her brain. The notorious Max was in fact Maximus, the legionary who had been instrumental in Cerdoc's death.

Focusing on her face, his eyes narrowed as he tried to place the slut who was glaring at him with such hatred, and then recognition dawned in his bleary gaze. 'Well, well, well,' he said, chuckling, 'if it isn't the little Iceni. You've come a long way since we last met. From battlefield to whorehouse.' He advanced on her, efficiently stripping off his clothes as he approached. Naked, he stood directly before her and thrust his face into hers. 'Well, bitch,' he whispered, 'it's time to finish what we started the last time we met.'

Branna flinched, but held her ground. She looked at him with disdain, taking in his hairy body, scarred chest and burgeoning belly. Then her eyes travelled lower, and she began to giggle uncontrollably. *So that* was what Bellinda had meant by his 'little problem'.

Taken aback, he glared at her. 'What are you laughing at?' he demanded.

'I'm laughing at you.' She pointed to the flaccid little member dangling between his thighs. 'Maximus?' she scoffed without caring. '*Minimus*, more like.'

His blow sent her reeling back across the couch, and before she had a chance to recover from it he was kneeling over her and binding her wrists with his belt. Twisting it viciously he fastened the loose end to the head of the couch, then stood up and smiled down at her. 'You're going to regret that remark,' he promised her quietly. 'I'm going to—!' He staggered and doubled up as Branna kicked out at him and her foot caught him square in the belly, knocking the breath out of him for an instant. He straightened up again, rubbing his stomach, then opened the cedar chest, took out the leather-covered bat, and laid it down on the table. Careful to avoid her feet this time, he leaned over and ripped her flimsy tunic away. She tried to wriggle out of his reach, but the belt around her wrists held her firmly in place. For a long moment he ran his hands greedily over her body, kneading her full breasts and pinching her nipples into hardness. Then he grinned cruelly, and flipped her over onto her stomach. The movement tightened the belt around her wrists even more, and left her completely helpless. 'Not so clever now, are you?' he goaded, eyeing the smooth curves of her bottom as he lifted the bat, and then brought it down with all his strength.

Branna screamed in the throes of a burning agony that seemed to turn her bones to ashes. Her buttocks jerked beneath the blow and she prayed to all the gods that he would not hit her again, but her hope was in vain. He brought the leather-covered bat down again, and her cheeks jumped and quivered beneath the impact.

'I'll teach you,' he panted, lifting his arm a third time.

Burying her face in the cushions, she clenched her buttocks against the coming onslaught, which was a mistake. This time when the blow fell it hurt twice as much, and she shrieked again. And then nothing existed but the consuming agony as he kept beating her.

When he finally stopped he ran a hand over her scarlet bottom, obviously enjoying the way she flinched beneath his touch. Then he flipped her over onto her back again, and smiled evilly down at her beauty and helplessness. 'That's certainly knocked the fight out of you,' he gloated with satisfaction.

She tried to kick him again, but the movement was feeble and caused her even more pain. He then grabbed her ankles and secured them to the couch. Now she was spread-eagled before him, completely unable to resist him as he bent over and greedily licked and sucked her breasts. Then he straightened up and walked over to the chest again. He returned holding the huge carved penis, and the short chain whose use she had been unable to fathom. But she soon found out what it was for, shrieking as he clamped the ends to her swollen nipples and sent even more pain lancing through her already tortured flesh - pain, and its mysterious companion, pleasure...

Branna whimpered as insidious tendrils of perverse excitement began uncoiling through her pelvis as her pussy moistened traitorously. Then she gasped as he roughly parted the lips of her vulva, and slid the large carved cock inside her. His upper lip curled back from his teeth as he began moving it in and out, slowly and carefully at first, then faster and harder, sinking it so deep inside her she caught her breath every time. She saw the flaccid cock between his hairy thighs twitching to life as he watched her unwilling response to the artificial penis, and when he was semi-erect he left the dildo buried inside her and straddled her shoulders, thrusting his prick in her face.

'Suck it, bitch,' he commanded hoarsely. She tried to turn her face away, but he seized her by the hair and fed himself between her lips. The more she resisted him the stiffer he grew, until she could hardly breathe past his swollen head. Leaning back he began to move the dildo in and out of her wet pussy again as he possessed her mouth, and moaning around his shaft, she closed her eyes as she gave herself up to the sensations coursing through her.

She sucked him greedily, running her tongue teasingly around his head as he pulled out, and slid deep between her lips again. He groaned, and she felt him swelling to the point where she nearly gagged on him as he started pumping his hips urgently in her face. The discomfort only intensified her excitement, however, making her suck him even harder, and his cock jerked and pulsed against her tongue as his salty seed spurted against the roof of her mouth. With another groan he slipped out of her, pulled the dildo from her pussy, and slumped down beside her on the couch.

Tears shimmered from beneath Branna's lashes onto her cheeks as she realised what she had just done. This was the man who had killed her beloved Cerdoc, and she had just... a sob escaped her.

'Stop snivelling and pour me a drink, whore,' he said impatiently, untying her wrists and pushing her off the couch with his foot so she could obey him.

She fell heavily to the floor, and as she struggled to get up her hand landed on the dagger he had dropped. Her fingers closed instinctively around the hilt, and it felt good in her hand...

'Where's my wine?' he demanded, looking down at her from beneath half-closed eyelids.

'Waiting for you in Hades,' she said quietly, and smiled triumphantly as she rose above him and plunged the dagger deep into his heart. 'And this is for my beloved Cerdoc!'

He was dead in an instant, an expression of almost comical surprise on his face, and exultation rushed like warm wine through her blood at the sight of her vanquished enemy. She had avenged her lover's death, and now, at last, she could join him in the next world.

Wrenching the dagger out of the motionless Roman, she placed the bloodstained tip against her left breast, closed her eyes, and pressed...

The point had just pierced her skin when a strong hand grabbed her wrist from behind. She wailed in frustration as the weapon was wrenched from her clutch and skidded across the floor as Catus flung it away. She followed it longingly with her eyes, until a sharp slap brought her head up and she found herself staring into Dolorosa's furious face.

'You stupid, stupid girl!' she screeched. 'You've killed him! Do you realise what that means?'

'I don't care,' Branna said with calm defiance. 'Why should I care? He deserved to die. They can tear me into a thousand pieces now, for all I care. I have finally avenged my lover's death, and that is all that matters.'

'And they *will* tear you to pieces,' Dolorosa hissed, her face livid, and then suddenly her expression changed and became thoughtful. 'If they find out, that is,' she said slowly. 'Who's to know he didn't leave here and go drinking somewhere else? The alleys of Rome can be dangerous places at night.' She bent and picked up the dead man's clothes, appropriating his purse in the process. 'We'll burn these, and *that*...' she glanced disdainfully at the corpse. 'That can go in the *cloaca maxima* with the rest of the shit.' Her thin lips twisted into a vicious smile. 'And he'll be in good company there. I've heard that's where Nero disposes of the unfortunates who don't survive the nightly riots.

'And as for you,' she went on, her smile disappearing as she turned back to Branna, 'I'll dispose of you elsewhere, and just be grateful I've saved your pathetic skin.'

'Saved your own pathetic skin, you mean,' the young beauty retorted boldly. 'And your investment.' Her top lip curled. 'Who would want to come here if it got out that a client had been murdered? That would put a damper on your trade real fast.'

'Get the little bitch out of here before I kill her myself,' Dolorosa snapped at Catus. 'Lock her in her room, and make sure she stays there. I'll deal with her in the morning.' She nodded at the body. 'Then come back here with one of the others and get rid of that before it starts to stink and someone sees it.'

Muttering beneath his breath, Catus hustled Branna back along the corridor, pushed her inside her *cubicula*, and slammed the door closed.

For a few minutes she paced the floor like a caged tigress, then the shock began to wear off and exhaustion pushed her back across her pallet, where she fell into a dreamless sleep.

It seemed only a few moments later that Dolorosa shook her awake again. 'On your feet,' the old woman hissed, 'and get yourself dressed. I want you out of here before you can do any more damage.'

Numbly, Branna slipped on her old tunic beneath Dolorosa's watchful eye, and then she followed the old hag downstairs. She was hustled out of the house, and marched through the streets with Dolorosa walking on one side of her and Catus on the other. They were heading towards the amphitheatre, but when they reached it, instead of walking towards the arena seating they turned down into the winding maze of corridors beneath it. Branna held her breath against the stench of old blood, and the animal scent of beasts in cages. At last they reached a small, whitewashed room where an elderly man was writing something on a scroll. He laid down his stylus and looked enquiringly up at them as they entered.

'This is the girl I sent you the message about,' Dolorosa told him. 'How much will you give me for her?'

The old man looked Branna over, and named a sum.

Dolorosa spat on the floor, and named a higher price. They haggled briskly for a few minutes, before reaching an amicable agreement. The money was counted out, and Dolorosa scraped it greedily into her purse. Then, as she turned to leave, she stuck her face in Branna's and grinned maliciously. 'Too good for my house, were you, slut? Well, we'll soon see how you enjoy being a circus whore.' Her mocking laughter echoed along the corridors as she and Catus made their way out of the amphitheatre.

With Dolorosa's final taunt ringing in her ears, Branna turned apprehensively back to the old man. He had picked up his stylus again and was carefully adding the sum he had paid Dolorosa to the list of figures on the scroll. Once he had finished, he stood up and nodded. 'Right,' he said briskly. 'Let's get you to your new quarters.'

Branna stared at him in disbelief that he could treat another human being like a pair of sandals he had just bought, and yet she knew she should not be so surprised. This was the arena, in which death itself was a cheap commodity. One more life made no difference whatsoever. The only difference between her and those who fought out on the hot sand was that their bodies were killed, whereas it was her spirit that would die a little more each day with every meaningless sexual bout her heart fought against. Theirs was an arena of blood. Hers was an arena of shame.

CHAPTER 9

Branna's room was little more than a tiny underground cell with stone walls and a threadbare pallet lying in one corner. As they passed the adjoining cells she glimpsed other girls, hard-faced and shop-worn, and when her new owner left her, he did not even bother to lock the door behind him. There was nowhere for her to go. Even if she attempted to escape, she would be stopped long before she made her way out of this underground warren. Lying down across the hard pallet, Branna buried her face in her hands, and wept.

'Welcome to the underworld,' a mocking voice declared, and she looked up to see a dark-haired girl smiling down at her. 'Cheer up, love, at least we've got food in our mouths and a roof over our heads. It's tough to begin with, but you'll get used to it. And you never know, one of the lads might take a fancy to you and keep the rest of the buggers off for a while.' She shrugged. 'Mind you, these infatuations don't last very long, so enjoy them while you can. But a pretty girl like you shouldn't have any trouble finding a protector. Even Cennus might take you, if you're really lucky.'

'Cennus?' she asked gingerly.

The girl looked at her as if she was retarded. 'Where have you been, love, out in the sticks? Cennus the Barbarian, the toast of Rome. More than a hundred bouts and he's never been defeated once.' She winked. 'He's got fine ladies queuing up all over the place to pay for his talents.' Her salacious grin was touched with envy. 'He must have made a fortune by now. The rumours say he bought his freedom ages ago. He could walk away whenever he likes, but he keeps on fighting. I think he enjoys the killing.'

The image of some hulking bloodthirsty brute entered Branna's head, and she tried to push it away. So this was what she had to aspire to, being the plaything of a man like that in the hope it would protect her from others not quite so bad? Dolorosa had been right, the *lupanar* was a girls' school compared to this place.

'Anyway, you'll soon find out what it's like,' the arena whore went on blithely. 'The games are on this afternoon, and they're like wild animals when they come in after being out on the sand. If I were you, I'd try and get a bit of sleep now and build your strength up for later. Believe me, you're going to need it.' And with that warning, she sauntered out of Branna's cell.

Sleep was the last thing on her mind as horrific images of the coming ordeal haunted her. Covering her ears with her hands against the noise filtering into her subterranean cell from the arena over her head, she closed her eyes and rocked back and forth, desperately trying to squeeze the dreadful pictures out of her head.

Gradually she became calmer, and entertained herself trying to make out individual sounds, which gave her something to concentrate on other than her fears. There were shouts and cries, the clatter of running sandaled feet, the clanging of bars, and the outraged screams and roars of the great cats as they were transferred to the cage that would take them into the arena. The machinery of death was efficiently in motion. She could even trace the passage of time by the noises above her, and the periods of relative quiet before it all began again. She listened to the dull sound of thousands of feet, and the drone of thousands of voices, as the audience kept making its way in and out of the tiers of seats. There was always a loud roar when a bout ended, followed by a pregnant silence before a fresh slaughter began. She sat hugging herself and shuddering occasionally as the sounds of death ebbed and flowed above her through the endless afternoon.

Then a different noise brought her back to her own sorry situation. Feet were approaching down the corridor towards her cell, and she could hear the sound of male voices and coarse laughter. She cowered back on her pallet as the door was flung open.

There were three of them. Flushed with success, they stood on the threshold grinning at her, their loincloths stained with sweat and blood. Her nose wrinkled in disgust and she looked frantically from one face to another, searching their expressions for even the smallest trace of kindness, but she found only a wild, brutish excitement.

'Well, don't just sit there gawping, girl,' one of the gladiators snapped his fingers at her. 'Get your clothes off and your legs spread, we're here to celebrate!'

She edged away from them until her back came up against the cold stone of the wall. They were in the cell now, and fanning out around her like animals stalking their prey. Laughing, the one who had spoken feinted towards her, and chuckled as she flinched away from him. He turned and grinned at his friends. 'We've got a wild one here, eh lads? But we'll soon tame her.'

Branna flew at him, her fingers curled into rigid claws. Her nails dug into his face, leaving in their wake livid bleeding furrows down each of his cheeks.

He swore beneath his breath and his grin vanished. 'You little bitch,' he said quietly, as though surprised by the assault. 'You'll pay dearly for that.'

Undeterred she lunged at him again, but this time he was ready for her. He caught her wrists and twisted her arms behind her back, trapping them in one large fist while with the other hand he grabbed the neck of her tunic and ripped it off her. His good humour restored by the sight of her naked body, he winked at his mates and pulled her against him, his free hand plunging between her thighs as he brought his mouth down over hers. He thrust his thick wet tongue into her mouth and she nearly gagged on his kiss, gasping for breath as she wrenched her head away, but her struggles merely aroused him. When she tried to kick him he laughed and deliberately fell backwards onto the pallet, dragging her with him so she lay helplessly across his lap.

'You've got to show them you're the boss,' he said to his comrades, running his hand appreciatively over her tight bottom. 'And the best way to do that is with a good spanking.' He lifted one meaty hand and brought it down with a smart smack on her clenched cheeks.

She squealed with outraged pain and wriggling frantically in an effort to escape his clutches. Tears of rage sprang into her eyes as his friends laughed, and twisting her head around, she bit the stout arm holding her down. Now it was his turn to gasp with pain as he clutched himself, cursing.

'What's wrong, Faestus?' one of his mates asked mockingly. 'I thought you were going to show her who was boss. Too much for you to handle, is she? Step aside and let a real man show you how it's done.'

'Get away, she's mine!' Breathing heavily, Faestus turned his attention back to Branna, and when his hand came down again she howled beneath the force of the blow. All his strength was behind it, and the flesh of her buttocks trembled beneath the shock of the impact, which left the imprint of his hand bright red against her skin. 'I'll teach you, you little slut,' he said through clenched teeth as his hand swept down again and again. She shrieked and writhed on his lap, and felt his cock swelling against her belly as his excitement mounted.

'That's the stuff, Faestus,' his friends cheered him on. 'You give it to her good and proper!'

'I'll give it to her all right.' He brought his hand down one final time, and then shoved her off his lap. As she tried to sit up he hauled her back onto the pallet, spread her legs, and began fumbling beneath his loincloth. His penis sprang out, heavy and swollen, and he stroked it swiftly. Then she groaned as he held her down with one hand and eased two fingers into her pussy. When he pulled them out they were slick with her juices, and he smiled. 'Well, look at this my friends, it seems our little whore has a taste for the rough stuff.'

Branna closed her eyes in humiliation as her lower body throbbed with a mixture of pain and desire. Once more her treacherous flesh was betraying her spirit.

He used her wet heat to lubricate the tip of his shaft, and then he gripped her hips, pulled her towards him, and penetrated her.

Sighing, she felt him sink the full length of his erection so deeply into her pussy that his balls rolled against her bottom, sending more bolts of exquisite torment through her. He withdrew, and then sank down again, smiling as he watched his thick, glistening cock sliding in and out of her tight little slot. The enticing sight was too much for him, and as his friends roared their encouragement he began thrusting frantically, his head thrown back and his mouth gaping open. She writhed beneath him, arching her back so her hips met his, and then cried out with pleasure as she felt him ejaculate violently inside her.

After a short while the gladiator rolled off her, completely spent.

'Shift yourself,' one of his friends grumbled, nudging him aside with his sandal. 'It's my go, now.'

'It's mine, you mean.' The third man reached for his cock and pulled it out from beneath his loincloth. '*You* can wait.' He waggled his erection back and forth. 'I'm going to ram this so far up her arse, she'll taste it in the back of her throat.'

'We can both go then,' the other man suggested impatiently. 'You can ream her arse while she sucks me off.'

'I don't think so,' said an icy voice from the doorway.

'Push off, mate,' said one of them. 'You can wait your turn like everybody else. She's a hot little piece, and there's plenty for everyone...'

Then the man's crude chuckle became a shriek of pain as he was pulled back away from the pallet and flung against the opposite wall. Wide-eyed, he stared at the helmeted man standing before him. 'Cennus!' he gasped, his face blanching. 'I'm sorry, my friend, I didn't know it was you.'

His organ immediately shrivelled and he covered himself quickly, edging towards the door of the cell as he did so. Faestus and the other man had already scurried away, the sounds of their retreating sandals echoing down the corridor, and with a weak smile, he took to his heels after them.

Dazed by the sudden turn of events, Branna stared up at the stranger, suddenly aware of the picture she must make sprawled inelegantly on the pallet. She sat up, and tried to cover her nakedness with the torn remnants of her tunic while glaring up at the newcomer with as much dignity as she could muster.

'Well,' she goaded derisively, 'aren't you going to take your turn, too?'

Lifting his helmet, the stranger stared down at her with pained blue eyes. 'No, Branna, I'm not,' Cerdoc replied sadly, and turning without another word, he left her cell.

Utterly stunned, Branna stared after him, her face frozen in shock and disbelief. This must be some ghastly trick of the gods. It could not be Cerdoc. Cerdoc was dead. She had seen his lifeless body with her own eyes.

Yet he had been far too solid to be some shade from the underworld. Her mind raced back to that dreadful day when she had watched him fall beneath a wave of Roman soldiers, and seen his seemingly lifeless and bloodstained body lying across the grass. Perhaps he had not been dead after all, merely beaten into unconsciousness. That would make more sense than believing he had come back from the dead to torment her.

Her racing thoughts were interrupted by the entry of the dark-haired girl who had spoken to her earlier. 'By all the gods!' her visitor exclaimed, leaning against the doorframe and looking at Branna with reluctant admiration. 'You must be *very* good. Four men fucked in less time than it takes to pluck a chicken, and one of them the great Cennus himself.'

Ignoring the backhanded compliment, Branna went straight to the point. 'What do you know of Cennus?' she demanded urgently. 'Tell me! Tell me everything you know!'

Taken aback by her vehemence the girl recoiled slightly, and then shrugged. 'Who cares?' she asked cynically. 'One gladiator is much the same as another. Where do *any* of them come from?'

Branna was across the room in an instant, and shaking the whore violently by the shoulders. 'I said tell me about him!' she repeated, her eyes glinting dangerously.

'All right, all right!' the girl objected loudly, pulling herself free. 'Keep your hair on.' She paused as she tried to remember the various rumours she had heard. 'Well, I think he's from one of those little islands in the arse-end of nowhere, you know, one of those distant outposts full of barbarian tribes with unpronounceable names.'

'Yes, I do know,' Branna said, calming a little as her mind raced. That would account for the name 'Cennus' as well - Iceni, Icenus, Cennus. It would be far easier for the Romans to get their slovenly tongues around that than around a noble name like Cerdoc. Then suddenly everything fell into place like the pieces of a terrible puzzle. He had fought like a cornered wolf, and the Romans, for all their faults, were warriors too, and respected courage in others. They also had an eye for the main chance. Someone had seen the opportunity to make a few extra *sesterces* off Cerdoc, and he had been sold into slavery. Her heart leapt. At least he was alive! Her beloved Cerdoc was alive!

But her joy was short-lived, and immediately replaced by a black despair. They had both been sold into slavery, but there the similarity of their fates ended.

Their paths had taken them in very different directions. He had gone on to fight his way to freedom and become the toast of Rome. Yet what had she become? She had become a whore in the arena, the scum of the city. He had seen her lying naked with her legs spread open and another man's come smouldering in her pussy. Why on earth would he want her now?

Heartsick, she turned away from the girl who was eyeing her curiously, spread herself across the filthy pallet again, and closed her eyes. There was nothing left for her now but death.

For the next few days not a morsel of food or drink passed Branna's lips. When the other girls tried to coax her to eat and drink she simply turned her head away and willed herself to die. She lost weight and became light-headed, and she knew it would not be long. She was smiling as she drifted off into darkness...

Someone was shaking her urgently by the shoulders, so reluctantly she opened her eyes and tried to focus on the anxious face looming above her. 'Cerdoc?' she murmured drowsily, trying to lift her hand to caress his beloved face. 'What are you doing here in the underworld? I thought you were still alive.'

'I am,' he said, 'and so are you. Here, drink this.'

She felt herself being lifted and cradled, and a goblet of sweetened wine was placed gently against her lips. Too weak to fight, she allowed the liquid to trickle down her throat, and felt its warmth spreading through her body. 'No,' she wailed softly, too weak to raise her voice as she tried to knock the reviving wine away. 'I don't want to live...'

'But I want you to live,' Cerdoc said firmly. 'You are my betrothed. How can I go on if I at last find you only to lose you again?'

She stared up at him in astonishment; not daring to hope this was not just a wonderful dream. 'B-but, I thought you hated me,' she stammered. 'You walked away without a backward glance.'

'Only to stop myself from killing your tormentors,' he said grimly. 'Killing is only acceptable when there's an audience... I love you, Branna, I've never *stopped* loving you.'

'But how can you?' she demanded bitterly. 'I'm nothing but a cheap whore, remember?'

'A whore chooses to be a whore, you were a slave,' he corrected her. 'A slave has no choices. I have been a whore, too.'

'But you are free now,' she said dully.

'And you are, too. Where do you think I've been these last few days? Look.' He fumbled in his tunic, and produced a scroll.

She stared at it blankly.

'It's your certificate of manumission,' he explained. 'I bought your freedom.' He smiled down at her gently. 'Of course, as a good wife I expect you to spend the rest of your life slaving for me.' He scooped her up in his arms. 'Now let's get you out of here and back to my apartments.'

The next few days were sheer bliss for Branna. To walk abroad as a free woman without having to look over her shoulder, knowing that never again would she be forced to do anything against her will, was almost too much for her to take in after being a helpless slave for so long.

And the nights were even better than the days as she snuggled against Cerdoc and they planned their future together. Her only complaint was that he had not yet made love to her. Was the thought of all those other men still standing between them?

'One last bout and we can leave this place,' he promised her. 'We can go home, buy a little farm somewhere, and start over.'

Cold fear touched her heart at the thought of his fighting again, but she held her tongue. The gods would not be so cruel as to tear them apart again now; she felt it in her bones. Yet when the day arrived she bade him farewell with terror in her heart.

'Here,' he said as he left, 'I don't want you sitting alone worrying. Go out and buy yourself something to pass the time.'

She stared in astonishment at the bag of gold coins he handed her. 'It is too much!' she protested.

'We have enough, and more,' he smiled. 'Now go and do as you're told, woman.'

In the marketplace she wandered from stall to stall trying to distract herself from the thought of Cerdoc fighting on the hot sand of the arena. She did not know what to buy. She had clothes aplenty now, and even jewels. Then a thought hit her, and she quickly hailed a passing litter.

'What can I do for you, my lady?' Dolorosa simpered. Then her calculating old eyes moved up from her visitor's fine dress to her face. 'What are you doing here?' she gasped, taking a confused step back.

'I have come to buy myself a whore,' Branna said curtly.

'Oh so, that's why your heart wasn't in your work,' the hag crowed. 'Your tastes lie,' she winked, 'elsewhere.' Then she suddenly became businesslike. 'Who do you fancy? Bellinda? Nubia?'

'No, Tallis,' Branna replied, 'and I don't want to buy her for the afternoon, I want to buy her freedom, so fetch the scribe as well.'

'That'll cost you,' Dolorosa warned her.

'I think not,' Branna smiled. 'Did I mention I was betrothed to Cennus? He would be displeased if you were to try and take advantage of me.'

Dolorosa turned a strange shade of green. 'All right, all right,' she grumbled. 'You can have her for what I paid, but not a *denarii* less.'

'Done. Now bring her here. I haven't got all day.'

'There,' Branna said when the documents were all signed. 'You're a free woman now, Tallis. What do you want to do, come back home with us?'

Tallis blushed, and glanced at the young scribe, Cassus, who smiled back at her adoringly. 'If you don't mind, Branna, I'd rather stay here,' she announced. 'Erm... Cassus wants to marry me. All that talk about killing Romans and then I go and fall in love with one of the bastards.' Her expression became anxious. 'You don't mind do you, Branna?'

'You're free now,' her friend told her. 'You can do as you like.' She kissed Tallis on the cheek. 'Just be happy, that's all I ask.' She looked at Cassus. 'And *you*, look after her, or you'll have me to answer to.'

'I will,' he promised fervently. 'I will.'

Back in Cerdoc's apartments all her fears rushed back to haunt her.

Where was he? He should have been back from the arena by now.

She paced back and forth, biting her lip in growing anxiety. Perhaps she had been wrong and the gods were even crueller than she could ever have imagined. Perhaps his lifeless body was even now being dragged from the arena by the heels...

Darkness had fallen by the time he finally arrived, his breath smelling of wine, and by then she was beside herself with fury born of terror. 'You bastard!' she shrieked, beating his powerful chest with her fists. 'I thought you were dead! I thought you were dead!'

He caught her raised hands, twisted them behind her back and pulled her close so her breasts were crushed against him.

His mouth came down on hers, forcing her lips apart, and his tongue sought hers hungrily. His cock hardening and digging into her belly, he pushed her down across the couch, pulled up her tunic, and feverishly sought the soft warmth between her thighs. Running a finger down her cleft he parted her like a ripe fig, and plunged his digit into her wet heat. She moaned as he finger-fucked her, watching her face as her mouth opened and her eyelids fluttered with pleasure.

Then he took out his cock and she moaned at the sight of it. His beautiful penis was swollen and ready for her, and she gasped with joy as it slid inside her. She gripped his buttocks, arching against him and feeling his muscles clench as he thrust himself into her.

He took her savagely, exorcising the memory of those who had gone before him, and together they gasped and shuddered to a blinding climax, after which they lay peacefully in each other's arms on the couch.

'Now you're truly mine again,' he said, stroking her face tenderly.

The following morning Branna awoke to the sound of furtive whispers and movements.

'About time, too,' Cerdoc scolded, smiling down at her. 'I've been working since dawn.' She stared at him uncomprehendingly. 'We're leaving today. It's all in hand.' A loud clatter turned his smile rueful. 'Well, almost,' he corrected himself. 'If those idiots don't break everything we possess before they load it on the cart.'

Hurrying into her clothes, Branna stepped out into the bare apartment, just in time to see a man stagger out bent over beneath the weight of a sack-wrapped vase.

'We'll take our personal things on a packhorse,' Cerdoc informed her through a mouthful of bread and cheese. 'Don't stand there gawping, woman, get yourself organised.' He shook his broad shoulders as if a fly had crawled across his skin. 'The sooner we shake the dust of this place from our feet, the better.'

Smiling happily, Branna ran to do as she was told.

They had almost reached the outskirts of the city when they were brought to a halt by a jeering mob streaming towards one of the gaol-houses.

'What's going on?' Cerdoc demanded, grabbing one of the men rushing by.

'Some bitch is being done for adultery!' he shouted. 'Seems she'd been sneaking off to the *subura* for fun and games and somebody tipped off her old man and he caught her. Well, she'll have her fill today.' He shook himself free and ran off eagerly.

'I want to see this,' Branna said, kneeing her horse so it forced its way through the crowd.

Peering through the barred window of the gaol-house, she saw Lavinia, naked and squawking with outrage, as a one-eyed beggar pushed her down and proceeded to ram his cock up her arse while the jeering onlookers egged him on.

As soon as he had finished with her two other old beggars took his place, one mounting her from behind while the other one shoved his cock in her mouth. Together they rode her while she squealed, and the crowd of men in the doorway tossed a dice for their turn.

Branna smiled. Her letter to Marcus Cornelius had worked. There would be no more ordering slaves about for Lavinia now. By the time sunset came and the scum of Rome had finished with her, it would be her old mistress's turn to whore for a living.

Wheeling her horse round she smiled at Cerdoc. 'Come,' she said, heading towards the gates and their future. 'We're going home!'

Thanks for reading!

www.ingramcontent.com/pod-product-compliance
Lightning Source LLC
Chambersburg PA
CBHW060943120626
46557CB00003B/1114